# Christmas in Transylvania

# *Christmas in Transylvania*

## A DEADLY ANGELS NOVELLA

# SANDRA HILL

AVONIMPULSE
*An Imprint of HarperCollinsPublishers*

Excerpt from *Vampire in Paradise* copyright © 2014 by Sandra Hill.
Excerpt from *Kiss of Pride* copyright © 2012 by Sandra Hill

EPub Edition OCTOBER 2014 ISBN: 9780062117557
Print Edition ISBN: 9780062117571

10 9 8 7 6 5 4 3 2 1

## Chapter 1

### Santa with fangs? . . .

"'Twas the night before Christmas, and all through the castle, not a creature was stirring, not even a bat—"

"Very funny!" Vikar Sigurdsson elbowed Karl Mortensen and almost knocked him off his kitchen stool. They sat side by side at the twenty-foot island counter in the huge castle kitchen. Karl's halfbrained rewording of the famous Yuletide story had been in response to Vikar's telling him that Alex, Vikar's wife, wanted them to have a traditional Christmas celebration this year, complete with holly, and decorated trees, and caroling, and feasts, and Santa Claus, and jingle bells, and gifts. All that ho-ho-ho nonsense.

'Twas enough to give a thousand-plus-year-old Viking vampire angel a headache!

Yes, Vikar lived in a lackwit, run-down castle (*more like falling-down, if you ask me, which no one ever does*) in lackwit Transylvania, and, no, not Transylvania, Romania. No, this was lackwit Transylvania, Pennsylvania (*Don't ask!*). As for bats, three years ago, when he'd begun the renovation of this hundred-plus-year-old, seventy-five room monstrosity, they'd had to first remove ten tons of guano. (*That's bat shit, to you uninformed.*) And they still hadn't eliminated all of the irksome creatures. Try sleeping at night to the sound of flapping wings in the turrets. Not that vangels (*Viking vampire angels, to you uniformed, again. Jeesh!*), like himself, weren't accustomed to the sound of flapping wings, but usually it was from St. Michael the Archangel, their heavenly mentor aka Pain In The Arse, whom they rudely referred to as Mike. (*When he was not around.*)

Vikar sipped at his long-necked bottle of beer. He and Karl were enjoying a midafternoon break from battle training down in the dungeons while Alex was off somewhere, probably dreaming up more of her honey-do jobs for him. *Not that I haven't told her more than once that they are more like honey-damn-don't chores.*

This is how the conversations usually went:

"*Honey, we need another bathroom on the fourth floor.*"

What was it with this "we" business. Women always used the "we" card when trying to convince men of one thing or another.

"*We already have two bathrooms on the fourth floor.*"

Vikar recalled a time when the only toilet facilities were wooden holes in an outdoor privy or a private spot in the woods. It had been cold enough betimes to turn a cock into an icicle.

"*I know. That's why we need three. Whew! It is so hot today. I think I'll go take a bubble bath. I don't suppose . . .*"

Alex knew sure as Eve tempted Adam that Vikar loved taking bubble baths with her. There was something about popping bubbles that appealed to the boy in him. Or the man.

*Face it, she pays no attention to my complaints. All she has to do is smile in that certain way, or hint at some sexual play, and I am Norse putty in her hands. Like this most recent, brilliant idea of hers. Holy clouds! She will be turning us all into ridiculous Santa Clauses. With fangs!*

He glanced over at Karl, who was sipping with distaste from a bottle of Fake-O. Vikar could have told him it was better to just chug the crap down and cleanse the palate with a bottle of beer. Fake-O was the synthetic blood vangels drank when they'd been too long from feeding during a mission.

Karl was a quiet kind of guy, the type who didn't feel the need to talk just to fill gaps in a conversation. A man's man, modern folks would say. He did the jobs that were handed to him with competency. No whining or complaints, like Vikar's brother Trond was wont to do, especially if it involved anything strenuous. Trond was a sloth if there ever was one although he was working to reform himself from his grave sin, as they all were.

There was a sadness about Karl, too, but not like Vikar's brother Mordr, who for centuries turned his sadness into a berserk madness, killing practically everything that got in his pathway. Mordr's sin had, of course, been wrath.

Vikar liked Karl.

Breaking the companionable silence, Vikar continued with his tirade, "It would be a sacrilege for us to celebrate such a commercial holiday, wouldn't it? We're practically angels."

"Practically?" Karl snorted. "You didn't look very angelic when I saw you coming out of your bedroom this morning."

Vikar grinned in remembrance. Three years he'd been wed, with more than a thousand years of experience in the bed arts under his belt, literally, and still his wife could surprise him.

"Besides, Vikings back in your time celebrated the holiday season, didn't you?"

*In my time?* Vikar mused. *Makes me sound ancient. Which I am. Still, I like to think of myself as my thirty-three human years.*

Karl was a Viking, too . . . all vangels were, by birth if not descent . . . but he was young for a vangel, having died only about forty years ago during the Vietnam War.

"Vikings celebrated the Yule season with great vigor. 'Tis true. Yule logs and gift giving. Feasts. Not a religious holiday, more a commemoration of the Winter Solstice. It was nothing like the secular extremes evident today. Even though we did, of course, have reindeer in the Norselands. None with a red nose, though, that I recall."

"It could be as secular or not, as you wish," Karl said. "Besides, Alex is right. Kids should experience the holiday season. And this will be the first Christmas that yours are old enough to understand."

*The traitor!* Vikar thought, at Karl's siding with his wife, but then he was probably right. Gunnar and Gunnora, Vikar and Alex's "adopted" twins, were three years old. For the past four days, ever since Thanksgiving . . . another chaotic holiday Alex had talked him into! . . . Gun and Nora had been yipping and yapping about Santa this and Rudolph that and jingle-belling 'til Vikar's head hurt. It had all started when they'd gone to something called "Black Friggsday" at the mall. Rather, "Black Friday." Betimes, he still fell into the old Norse words, like *Friggsday* for Friday, because, after all, despite being a vampire angel, he was a Viking at heart. *Which should be good enough reason to not have to be reminded to ever fall for that trap again.* "*Honey, would you drive us to the mall? Gun and Nora need new shoes. It will be fun.*" Hah! *If I never hear Alvin and the Chipmunks again, it will be too soon!*

"Did you celebrate Christmas when you were growing up?" he asked Karl.

The young man . . . even *though Karl had forty-two vangel years on top of his twenty-two human ones, Vikar still thought of him as young* . . . rarely spoke of his past. His situation had been unique amongst the vampire angels since he'd left behind a young wife who lived out her human years until she died two years ago at age sixty-three. Imagine staying the same age yourself but watching a loved one grow older and older, then perish of a wasting disease!

Karl smiled. A sad smile, Vikar noticed. "Yes. I grew up on a small farm in Minnesota, with a brother and two sisters. We were poor as church mice even though my dad worked from dawn 'til dusk milking cows and growing corn and hay. Mom had a big vegetable garden and put away hundreds of Mason jars filled with different things every fall. String beans, carrots, peas, corn, limas, beets, pickles, chowchow, peaches, pears, applesauce. If it grew, she preserved it.

"We had a Christmas tree, of course, with strings of ancient lights that were probably a fire hazard. And old ornaments. Homemade ones, too. We believed in Santa Claus, early on, anyhow. We even believed the old tale that animals talk on Christmas Eve. Many a night, us kids snuck out of the house to the barn to listen. I swore I heard old Bessie say, 'Moo-rry Christmas' one time." He laughed.

And Vikar laughed with him. It was a revelation, hearing Karl talk about his background. He hardly ever talked about himself.

"Mostly, our gifts were practical ones. Maybe a hand-knitted sweater or mittens or socks. Nuts, hard candies, and some fruit that was out of season for us, like nectarines, would be in our stockings, which we hung without fail over the fireplace."

*There are thirty fireplaces in this friggin' castle*, Vikar mused, and had a sudden horrifying image of stockings hanging from every one of them. Some of the younger vangels were often like children themselves and would sure as sin be wishing for gifts from the fat man in the red suit. Images of Armod, the sixteen-year-old vangel from Iceland, immediately came to mind. Armod fancied himself Michael Jackson reincarnated. (*You do not want to see a Viking vampire moonwalking! Trust me!*)

"Each of us only got one present," Karl continued.

Over the holiday, there could be as many as a hundred vangels in residence at the castle, especially if his brothers came with their contingents. Knowing Alex, she'd probably already issued invitations. Surely, he wouldn't be expected to go gift shopping for all of them. Would he? Vikar shuddered with mall tremors.

His headache felt as if it were growing. Maybe he was developing a brain tumor. Good idea. That might be sufficient excuse for Alex to get the Christmas bug out of her ... um, head.

"One gift only, but, man, it was always something special. I remember the year I got a BB gun."

"And your parents didn't worry that you would shoot your eye out?" Vikar asked, referring to the famous line from *The Christmas Story*, a movie some of his vangels loved.

"Nah! Growing up on a farm, we were used to hunting and stuff. I got to be a pretty good shot, too. That's why I was recruited to be a sniper in the Army, and—" Karl's words trailed off. He never spoke of his time in Vietnam, the time of his great sin. "Anyhow, there's nothing for a kid like those weeks leading up to Christmas. The smells of evergreens in the house and the baking. Ma made a dozen different kind of cookies, and pies, even homemade fruitcake. And the Christmas dinner was a regular feast, with turkey and stuffing, mashed potatoes, gravy, rutabaga and corn, string bean casserole, cranberry sauce, fresh fruit salad, and rolls, warm from the oven dripping with butter."

At the mention of all that baking and food preparation, their cook's head shot up. Lizzie Borden had had been sitting at the far end of the counter, skimming through a recipe book. He hadn't realized they'd been speaking so loud. And, yes, it was *that* Lizzie Borden, who wielded her axe these days chopping vegetables and beef carcasses. Lizzie was the most sour-dispositioned woman Vikar had ever met. She exchanged a look with him that said loud and clear, "Don't even think about it!"

Karl hadn't noticed Lizzie's expression. Instead, he was still lost in childhood memories. "The excitement, that's what I remember most. The anticipation of Christmas was almost as special as Christmas itself." He shrugged, as if helpless to explain it all.

Actually, he'd done a pretty good job, not of convincing Vikar that he should go all out with Christmas madness, as Alex's plan would surely be, but of showing a more simple view of the holiday. "Is the farm still there?"

Karl nodded. "I've not been permitted to make myself visible to any of my family, especially while Sally was still alive." He bit his bottom lip for a long moment before going on. "Mom died a long time ago, but my dad is still alive. Finally retired at eighty-nine. My little brother Erik works the land now. Quite a prosperous operation these days." He laughed. "I say little, but Erik is fifty-eight now, and has not just grandchildren, but one great-granddaughter."

Just then, Vikar heard the loud bang, bang, bang of little feet stomping down the uncarpeted back stairs. Laughing (Was there anything sweeter than the sound of a child laughing?), excited chatter (Do children know how to talk below a shout?), shrieking "I'm first, I'm first."

Gunnora rushed through the doorway of the servant's staircase, shoving her brother aside with a swing of her tiny hip. Her blonde braids were half-undone, and she had a dirt smudge on her freckled nose. "Papa, look what I found in the attic." She was carrying a wooden-soldier nutcracker almost as tall as she was. "Gimme a nut, Lizzie," she ordered.

"I'll give you a nut, you little tyrant," Lizzie muttered, and went back to reading her recipe book.

Close behind Nora was her twin, Gunnar, who carefully held a wooden stable, inside of which Vikar could see what appeared to be painted-wood Nativity figures. Gun put it on the floor and began to arrange the little statues of the Holy Family and animals. "I need some straw," he said to himself. "Betcha that Amish man at the farmers' market has some."

And then there was Alex, his wife, who could still make his heart (and other body parts) leap, despite their being married two years now. "Honey, wait 'til you see what I found for you," she said, placing a dust-covered box on the counter in front of him.

*Uh-oh. There is that* honey *again. Best I raise my shield and prepare for battle.*

Gun and Nora were jumping up and down with excitement. "Open it, Papa. Open it." And the gleam in Alex's eyes was much like that of a Norseman just home from a long trip a-Viking, offering some treasure or other to a loved one. Maybe she was not asking another favor of him but granting one. He would be open-minded.

"Thank you, love," he said graciously.

But then he saw what was inside and thought, *Screw open-minded.*

He said, "Holy shit!" before he could catch himself. Alex did not like him to use foul language in front of the children. But this required a *Holy shit!* if anything ever did. Inside the box was a moth-holed, old-fashioned Santa suit, with a black leather belt, big boots, and a ridiculous, peaked cap.

Just then, Nora let out a little squeal and set aside the nutcracker. Running over to the window facing the back courtyard, she said, "It's snowing! It's snowing!"

And Gun said, "Maybe we can make a snowman, just like Frosty."

And Alex, who was tone-deaf or close to it, burst out into song, "It's beginning to look a lot like Christmas."

And Karl said, "I'm outta here."

"Can I come with you?" Vikar asked.

"Hell, no, Mr. Scrooge!"

Once Karl was gone, and the children had gone off with a grumbling Lizzie to find some coal and carrots and a cap for Frosty, he and Alex were alone. He glanced pointedly at the open box, and said, "Surely, you don't expect me to . . . come on, Alex, sweetling . . . Santa with fangs? Ha-ha-ha."

She didn't laugh. Instead, she gave him that little secret Mona Lisa smile . . . and, yes, he had met the model for the Mona Lisa painting one time and knew exactly why she had been smiling. "Honey," Alex purred.

*Beware of women who purr.* "No, no, no!" he said. And he continued to insist, "No, no, no," until Alex yawned and mentioned taking a little nap. He did so enjoy afternoon "naps" with his wife.

Still, he protested, "A Viking Santa?"

Somehow, Alex managed to hop up onto his lap, straddling his hips. With arms looped around his neck, she said, "Please?"

"I will be the laughingstock of Vikings throughout this world and the other," he said on a groan of surrender.

Oddly, he found that he no longer cared.

## Chapter 2

*Vangel to the rescue . . .*

KARL HAD TO get away from the castle.

That was nothing unusual. There were always so many people around the vangel homeplace, it was hard to find a private spot to be alone. And Karl was a loner at heart.

At the present time, there were thirty-five or so vangels in residence. Sometimes, there could be up to two hundred although not so much anymore since Michael had commissioned Ivak to establish another headquarters in Louisiana, and plans were supposedly afoot for more satellite operations. When not out on a mission, vangels here usually helped Vikar with whatever latest restoration job was in progress. Painting, plastering, plumbing, whatever, it was never-ending. Or they hung out in one of the twenty-five bedrooms, or the family television room, or the library, or the dormitory, lounge, and weight rooms in the dungeon basement. It was like having dozens of annoying brothers and sisters. And they all loved nothing better than to stick their noses in each other's business. Viking busybodies!

*And now Christmas! The castle will be even more chaotic than usual. I'll be damned if I dress up like jolly ol' Nick because sure as sin Alex won't be satisfied with just one Santa. And I'll be damned if I sing Christmas carols. I could make anatomically correct Gingerbread Men and Women, though, like the ones Eric and I made when we were kids before Ma whipped our butts.*

The memory brought a smile to his face before he hopped in his ten-year-old pickup truck. Before turning on the ignition, he rubbed his hands over his bristly head in frustration. He'd kept his hair military short ever since 'Nam. Maybe it was time for a change.

But not today.

He often got in his pickup truck and just went out for a drive, or stopped at a greasy spoon for a cup of coffee, or on rare occasions parked on a hill overlooking one of the Amish farms outside of town and sat in his vehicle, watching the everyday activities of farm life. Pathetic, really.

But today was different. What was it with that diarrhea of the mouth he'd suddenly developed? Talking nostalgically about his childhood home and family like they'd been the friggin' Waltons or something? Pfff! Next he would be blabbing about his tour in 'Nam, at which point he would have to slit his own throat.

Yeah, maybe it was time for a new hairstyle. Time to rid himself of that last visible reminder of that horrible episode in his life, when he'd committed his great sin. Hah! He could wear a ponytail down to his ass, and that wouldn't change anything. The reminders were embedded forever in his brain.

He drove slowly down the long driveway that led through the hundred-acre property and nodded as Svein waved him through the electronic gate that had been erected last year. Security was extremely important, not just to keep out the tourists who flooded the whack-job town of Transylvania, but it was important that the location of the vangel command center be kept a secret from Jasper, king of all the Lucipires, their most hated enemy.

Lucipires were demon vampires, one of Satan's many tools, whose sole purpose was to kill evil people, or those about to commit some great sin, before their time, before they had a chance to repent. Those taken were not sent to Hell but to Horror, where Jasper and his minions tortured them until they turned into Lucies themselves.

Lucipires were the reason why vangels had been created to begin with. And humans, who had been guilty of some grave sin during their human life, like himself, were more than grateful for this second chance at redemption. It was either that or go south to that other place. Really south. Where it was hotter than Hades. Wait a minute. It *was* Hades.

Karl shook his head at the idiocy of making jokes with

himself. Next he would be talking to himself. And babbling like a moron. *Here's a news flash, Mortensen, you already did that.*

He passed the "Welcome to Transylvania" billboard, then St. Vladamir's Church, where the outdoor sign read, "God Loves All His Creations . . . Even You." He had to give the town credit. It had been a depressed, dying burg here in the boondocks until about seven years ago, when some enterprising fellow came up with the idea of jumping on the vampire bandwagon. Back then, the book *Twilight* had been published with great acclaim, and that *True Blood* series was just taking off.

They changed the name of the town to Transylvania, and every business developed a vampire slant, one dorkier than the other. The naysayers had predicted the vampire craze would die out, but thus far, that hadn't happened. Tourists swamped the town year-round, except for the coldest months, but even now the town council was planning some big Christmas bash that would draw vampire aficionados, despite the weather.

The good thing was that vangels, who'd taken over the long-abandoned, run-down castle up on the hill, built by a lumber baron a century or so ago, didn't stand out in the crowds here. Not even when they were wearing long cloaks to hide their weapons. The townfolks thought the castle was being renovated into a hotel.

Snow was coming down harder now. Big, fat flakes. Karl turned the windshield wipers on and amped up the heat as he passed slowly through town. He was wearing only an unlined denim jacket, and the temperature was dropping by the minute.

Here and there, Karl waved to people he knew. Well, not really "knew." Acquaintances. Vangels tried not to get too close to humans for fear of revealing their true selves.

Maury Bernstein, owner of Good Bites, who stood in the open doorway of his restaurant watching the snow come down, was probably wondering if it would affect his dinner crowd. There were at least twenty restaurants and bars serving food and drinks in the area. Everything from The Bloody Burger Joint to Drac's Dungeon to The Dark Side. A signature drink at most of the bars was called a "Bloody Fang."

Stella Cantrell was hanging a wreath on the door of Stinking Roses, a tiny shop that specialized in everything involving garlic. *Stinking rose* was another name for garlic, Karl had learned on moving here. Apparently garlic was supposed to repel vampires though the town's purpose was to attract them, of course. Personally, he liked garlic, in moderation. Anyhow, Stella's wreath had garlic bulbs adorning it as well as holly berries.

Other stores sold capes, fake fangs, crosses on heavy gold chains, even stakes, which could double for tomato-plant supports, and posters. Several T-shirt shops did a flourishing business with logos like "Fangbangers," "Got Blood," "Sookie Got Screwed," "Bitten," and so on. The adult video store had been forced to move last year to the outskirts of town by conservatives outraged at the vulgar titles in the window. They were probably right since tourists often brought kids with them, but the titles of some of them *had* been funny. Like *Ejacula, Intercourse with a Vampire, Fang Me, Bang Me,* or *Vlad Had a Really Big Impaler.*

Leaving the town proper, Karl headed west toward Penn State University though it was a good distance away. Two miles out of town, he passed the Bed & Blood Bed-and-Breakfast, run by an Amish couple, who were being shunned by their community. The husband made hand-carved specialty caskets that he sold on the Internet, probably the reason they were ostracized by their order. Alex was friends with them and bought lots of fresh produce there.

Karl had been feeling jumpy all day. The skin-crawling sensation he often got before a mission. Which was odd because there was no particular mission on the agenda as far as he knew. He'd quit smoking last month. That was probably what was affecting him so. Or maybe he needed a cup of coffee. Caffeine had the opposite effect on him as some folks. It tended to calm him down.

He pulled into the almost empty parking lot of Drac's Diner off Route 322. There was something . . . rather, someone . . . he needed to check on here.

The bell on the door tinkled when he entered. The only other customers were a couple in a back booth and a truck driver sitting at the far end of the counter having an early dinner. Other than the name of the diner, this place didn't do much to push the vampire theme, except during the high season, when the staff might don fake fangs. Their menu hadn't changed in years.

"Hey, stranger," the manager and co-owner, Jeanette Morgan, called out. "Coffee and a piece of apple pie?"

"Just coffee today, thanks."

He sat down at the counter, near the register, and straddled the stool. "Where's Faith today?"

Faith was a young waitress that worked here. A tiny bird of a woman who always looked frightened. She reminded him a little of his deceased wife Sally, except Faith was way thinner, and her blonde hair was always lank, and her blue eyes dull.

Jeanette rolled her eyes and leaned over the counter toward him. "She called in sick again today. I'm worried about her."

That prickly sensation on his skin turned pricklier. "Why?"

"She's being abused by that no-good bastard she lives with. Leroy Brown, named after that junkyard-dog song, no doubt. Can't hold a job or his temper. Never has two pennies to rub together but plenty for that souped-up Harley of his and for the booze. Meanwhile, she drives a twenty-year-old, rusted-out Volkswagen with bald tires. The jerk lives off Faith's piddly tips when he's unemployed, which is most of the time. Fashions himself some kind of heavy metal musician in local dives. Pfff! Heavy metal jackass, if you ask me!"

The fine hairs on the back of Karl's neck stood out with alarm. "What do you mean by abuse? Yelling, verbal insults, that kind of thing?"

"I wish! Not that making her feel like crap isn't his M.O., but he hits her, too. Last year, he broke her wrist.

One time, when he was really plastered, he carved his initials on her thigh."

Karl saw red, literally, for a moment. "Why does she stay with him if . . . never mind. I know about the abused-wife syndrome. Every TV shrink in the world talks about it."

"She's not his wife, thank God. But same as, I guess. Problem is that business slows down for us here during the winter, and her tips have been smaller. I suspect that Leroy the Loser thinks she's holding out on him. He usually hides any marks he puts on her, but last week I noticed finger marks on her neck. He's escalating. Poor Faith! She doesn't deserve this."

That was it! Karl stood abruptly, causing his coffee to splash over into the saucer. "Where does she live? I'll go check on her."

"Would you?" Jeanette asked hopefully. "I thought about calling the police, but a trooper who was in here yesterday told me they have to have cause for even knocking on a door, not just suspicions. And she has never filed a complaint, I don't think. These days, the law protects the perps as much as the victims. The trooper's words, not mine."

"What's the address?"

"I'm not sure. She lives in a small trailer park off the road between Reedsville and Belleville. Called Floral Heaven, or Floral Oaks, or some such thing."

Somehow, Karl would find her. "What's her last name?" he asked, finding it hard to believe he was off to rescue someone whose name he didn't even know.

"Larson. Faith Larson."

He reached for his wallet, about to pay for his coffee, when Jeanette waved his hand aside. "On the house, buddy. And, hey, would you please let me know what you find out, either way?"

"Sure," he said.

It was a fifteen-minute drive along Route 322 under normal circumstances, but today the snow continued to fall heavily, and the going was slow. Especially when he made the turnoff onto the two-lane Route 655 at Reedsville and kept getting caught behind one Amish buggy after another. They were picturesque as anything here in Big Valley, but when you were in a hurry, nothing but a nuisance. He took a deep breath and deliberately tamped down his anxious nerves, taking in the sights. One antique shop after another. Peachey's Meat Market, where Lizzie often bought whole carcasses of beef or pork or lamb, or fresh vegetables at the farmers' market in the summer months. The Rustic Log Furniture Barn. Brookmere Winery. A woodcarver and several fabric and quilt shops. Alex purchased many Amish quilts for the beds back at the castle. They were pretty and very expensive.

Finally, unable thus far to find any trailer park at all, he had to give up and ask for directions. He stopped and went into Dayze Gone Bye Carriage Rides, which offered tours of the Amish farms in better weather. There were no customers today, of course.

"Goot day!" said the Amish fellow, who wore the traditional plain clothes of his order, black pants and jacket, blue shirt, long beard, and hair that looked liked it had been cut with a bowl over the head. "Kin I help ya?"

Karl went up to the counter, and asked the young man, "Can you tell me where to find Floral Oaks Trailer Park, or maybe it's Floral Heaven?"

"Can't say I ever heard of . . . oh, ya mean Rose Haven. Ya gotta turn back t'ward the highway 'bout a mile or so. Turn right at Yoder's Orchard, then drive 'bout a quarter mile up the road."

"Thanks," he said, giving a little salute. Another thing he needed to stop doing.

He soon found the place, and what a pitiful excuse for a trailer park it was, too. About a dozen rusty old trailers with propane tanks outside for heat sat around in a cluster. Even covered with snow, their sorry condition couldn't be hidden. An old VW bug was parked in front of one of them, and, luckily, no motorcycle was in sight.

He knocked on the door, and, although he heard some music playing lightly in the background . . . a country music song by the sounds of it . . . no one answered the door. He knocked some more, "Open up, Faith. It's me, Karl Mortensen. Jeanette asked me to come check on you."

Finally, the door opened a crack.

And he was not prepared for what he saw. He, who'd seen more horrific sights in his short life than any man should, both in 'Nam and as a vangel fighting demon vampires, was shocked.

Faith's left eye was swollen shut. There was a black-and-blue handprint across her cheek. And her bottom lip looked as if it had been Botoxed all to hell, without the benefit of the pricey shots; a crack in the middle still oozed blood. Who knew how bad the rest of her was, the part hidden by the door?

"Jesus, Mary, and Joseph!" he muttered, and shoved the door wider.

"Hey, you can't just come in here and—"

"Try and stop me, sweetheart." Then, "Oh, honey, you need go to the emergency room or to a doctor."

She was wearing a short-sleeved PSU sweatshirt and loose jeans. Her feet were bare. She was a skinny little thing, which made the bruises on her arms more star-tling, and she kept one hand over her stomach, where Leroy had probably kicked her. He tried not to imagine initials carved on her thigh.

"NO!" she shouted with alarm. Then, more softly. "I can't go to a doctor or an emergency room. They're too expensive, and they'll want me to file a complaint." She stared at him for a moment. "You're the guy from the diner who always orders coffee and apple pie."

As if that mattered! "Why wouldn't you want the bas-tard arrested?"

"Because he would come after me when he got out, and it would be worse."

"Where is the junkyard dog now? Off beating on an-other helpless woman?"

"He went to the store. For beer."

That was all the asshole needed. More alcohol to fuel his rage, which translated to more beating up on the clos-est victim he could find. In other words, Faith.

"Let's get out of here then. Go pack a bag."

She shook her head. "I can't. He'll find me. He always does."

"Surely, there's a women's shelter that—"

"No! I've tried that before. He always, always finds me."

"Listen, this ends today. Unless you love the bastard and want to stay with him until he finally kills you."

"I don't love him," she spat out. "I haven't for a long time, but I have no choice. People like you, all high-and-mighty, think it's so easy to just walk out, but it isn't. It isn't!" she sobbed.

"It is now. I've got your back, and no one, NO ONE, is going to hurt you again."

She peered hopefully up at him through her one open, tear-misted eye. Tears also seeped from the closed eye, which probably burned like a bitch. "Where can I go?"

"With me?"

"Where?"

Oh, Lord! Was he really going to do this? "Back to my place. You'll be safe there." *I won't be, once Mike finds out, though. Ah, hell! What else can I do?*

She went into the tiny bedroom to pack, and he paced around the small space that was a kitchen, dining room, and living room combined. It was shabby as all get out but spotlessly clean. The most pathetic little Charlie-Brown-style tree sat on a windowsill. There was a small TV in the corner, but an electric guitar beside it that probably cost at least a thousand dollars. A man's high-end leather jacket hung from a wall peg, next to a threadbare, puffy pink jacket that probably came from Goodwill. The temperature inside was decidedly cool. They were probably out of fuel.

"Hurry up in there, Faith. The snow's coming down pretty hard, and we have a long drive back to the cas— back home." He went over to the kitchen counter and turned off the old Bakelite radio, on which Miranda Lambert was belting off something about not being able to go home. *Wanna bet?* he thought.

"I'm ready," she said, standing in the doorway with a battered, old-fashioned, hard-surface Samsonite overnight suitcase. She'd put on a pair of white sneakers, which would get wet just walking outside, but he wasn't about to ask her to change. He took the luggage out of her hand while she donned the pink jacket and topped it off with a fuzzy pink hat with a matching scarf, both having seen better days. She looked like a Pepto Pez.

Just then, they heard the sound of a motorcycle riding up the road, stopping outside, revving its motor in a display of pure masculine idiocy, then a male voice exclaiming, "What the hell?"

"Leroy, I presume?"

She nodded and made a small mewling sound like a whipped kitten. Her body began to tremble.

"Don't, Faith. He can't hurt you anymore."

"Yes, he can. He'll hurt you, too."

Karl made a snorting sound of disagreement. "I'd like to see him try."

"Oh, you should have never come. This is bad. Really bad."

The door flew open and banged against an interior wall, causing a framed print of the *Last Supper* to fall to the floor, its glass shattering.

A sign if he ever saw one.

"I knew it. You bitch! You've been fucking around on me all this time." Leroy was six feet of bodybuilder muscle, close to two hundred pounds, wearing a studded motorcycle jacket over a "Bang a Biker" T-shirt. Black jeans were tucked into heavy motorcycle boots.

"No, Leroy. It's not what you think. This is just a . . . a friend from the diner."

"Bullshit! You've been screwing a fuckin' jarhead, all the time tryin' to pretend you're Little Miss Innocent. You're a slut, that's what you are."

"You got it all wrong, man," Karl started to say.

"You! You!" Leroy sputtered, pointing a forefinger at Karl, spit flying. "Nobody fucks with my woman and walks away. You are dead meat!"

"Your woman? I didn't realize that you were married," Karl said, edging away from Faith to get a better position for when Leroy struck, which he surely would.

"Same as!" Leroy contended. "Tell him, Faith. Tell him you're mine."

Faith just whimpered, unable to speak.

Which infuriated Leroy even more. He fisted his hands.

It was obvious to Karl that Leroy was debating in that thick, testosterone-fueled brain of his whom to hit first, him or Faith.

Karl had other plans.

Leroy took up way too much space in this small trailer. Karl hated the image of a brute of this size and strength beating on a woman like Faith, who couldn't be more than five-foot-three and a hundred and ten pounds soaking wet. He could handle Leroy even though the ape had a good twenty pounds on him. *Wake up, Loser. You don't want to tick off a vangel.*

But wait. The smell of lemons filled the air, a sure signal to vangels and Lucies alike that this was an evil man, or one about to commit some evil. In Leroy's case, probably both. It was Karl's job as a vampire angel to try to redeem sinners like Leroy. To offer them a chance to change their bad ways. He'd like to sic a Lucie on Leroy instead and send him to the Horror he deserved.

Still, Karl said, "You don't want to do this, Leroy. Why not take a stand today? Turn a new leaf? I can help you."

"Suck my dick!"

*Okaaay!* Karl just smiled, he couldn't help himself.

Faith looked at Karl like he was crazy. She had to be thinking that her knight in shining armor riding in on a snow-white horse was actually a wuss in a Levi jacket driving an old pickup truck.

He had news for her. Not that he was any kind of a hero, but damn, some days it was good to be a vangel.

## Chapter 3

### *He wasn't G.I. Joe. He was better . . .*

Faith was terrified.

Leroy would kill her this time. Heck, he'd almost killed her two days ago, when he'd found the money she'd hidden from him so that she could order fuel.

And now she'd somehow gotten another person involved as well. She'd seen Leroy break a guy's jaw one time just because he'd parked his vehicle too close to Leroy's precious Harley in a bar parking lot.

"I think you should go," Faith told Karl.

"I don't think so, honey," Karl said.

"Honey?" Leroy roared, and raised his fists, about to charge.

Karl moved so fast, Faith couldn't believe her eyes. It was almost supernatural the way he was standing beside her one moment and behind Leroy the next with one hand twisting Leroy's left arm up to his shoulder blade and the other hand pressing against Leroy's thick neck so that Leroy was forced to raise his chin. Leroy was stunned, too, especially when Karl forced him to his knees.

"Faith, pick up your luggage and go outside. My truck is unlocked."

At first, she couldn't comprehend what was happening.

"Go!" he ordered.

Even as she began to move, she heard Leroy make a gurgling noise, and Karl moved his fingers from the front to the back of his neck, which he pinched, hard. And Leroy fell forward onto the thin carpet with a thud.

Most alarming of all, Karl appeared to have fangs coming out of his mouth. Noticing her watching him, he swiped a hand over his lips, and they were gone. She must have been mistaken. "Go!" he repeated.

Then it appeared as if he had wispy blue wings fluttering out of his back, like an angel. Her one eye was swollen shut, and her vision in the other eye must be impaired because when she blinked, the wings were gone, too.

*Fangs and wings? A vampire angel?* she thought with hysterical irrelevance. *All this battering from Leroy must have shaken something loose in my brain.*

Opening the door, she ran outside. The snow was coming down so heavily, she could hardly see. Making her way to the old pickup truck, she opened the passenger door, shoved her suitcase into the backseat, and climbed in the front, closing the door behind her. It was still fairly warm inside.

Sobbing, she pulled a tissue from her jacket pocket. Dabbing at the bruised eye, which burned from the salty tears, she wondered how her life had gotten so messed up. She was almost thirty years old and had no future to speak of. Despite having grown up in one foster home after another, she'd managed to graduate from high school with honors, and she'd had a good job at Penn State as a secretary, was even taking some college courses toward a degree.

But that was before she'd met Leroy five years ago. Everything in her life could be measured that way, it seemed. Before Leroy. After Leroy. BL. AL.

The driver's door opened abruptly, and Karl jumped in. "Brrr!" he said. "I think the temp dropped ten degrees since I got here."

What could she say to that? There were more important things, for sure. "Is Leroy dead?" she asked.

There was surprise in his pale blue eyes as he turned his head to stare at her. "Do you want him to be?"

"Of course not." But she did want him gone. Out of her life. And, yes, she had to admit, there had been times she'd wished him dead. Too many times.

"No, sweetheart, he's not dead, although he probably deserves to be. I just pinched a nerve in his neck, causing him to black out. He'll be on his feet in no time."

"Good," she said. But what she thought was, *Leroy will surely kill me now. And Karl, as well.* There was no turning back the clock, though. What was done was done. "We better get out of here then, before he wakes up."

He turned on the ignition, and blessed heat blew out,

filling the cab of the truck like a warm cocoon, especially with the windows covered with snow. Backing up, he turned around and drove down the lane toward the highway, the windshield wipers swishing back and forth. It was beginning to look like a real blizzard.

"Everything is going to be all right," he told her.

She couldn't imagine how it could be. She didn't even know the man, but she had to admit, she did feel safe for the moment. "Thank you," she said softly.

"My pleasure," he said with a grin.

He really was a nice-looking guy. A lot younger than her, of course. Probably in his early twenties. Although he had a military haircut; so, maybe he'd served in the armed forces and was older than he looked. "How old are you?" she asked.

He grinned some more. "Older than you could imagine. How about you?"

"Twenty-nine. Almost thirty."

"No shit! I mean, no kidding! You look about sixteen."

She shrugged. "I always did, even before I lost some weight."

He arched his brows as if to say she'd lost more than "some weight."

"Are you in the Army or something?"

"Or something," he replied without thinking, then added, "I used to be one of Uncle Sam's finest. No more."

"I could tell—"

"Don't talk," he advised then. "Your lip is bleeding."

She used the tissue in her hand to blot the moisture where her lower lip had cracked open again.

Karl reached over and turned on the radio. The air was suddenly filled with George Strait singing that old song, "I'll Be Home for Christmas."

"Damn! Christmas music already!" Karl swore and was about to change the station.

"No. Leave it on. I like that song." She leaned her head against the headrest and let the warmth and the music and sudden peace envelop her. Just before she fell asleep, a thought occurred to her, *I wonder where I'll be this Christmas.*

### Home, Sweet Home . . . or is it, Castle, Sweet Castle? Whatever! . . .

By the time Karl turned onto 777 Sayers Drive, the lane leading up to the castle, he had come up with a plan.

He would somehow park in the back lot, sneak Faith into the castle, go up the back staircase, one meant for servants when the monstrosity had been built, to the third floor, where his bedroom was located overlooking the rear courtyard. Once there, he would somehow assess Faith's medical condition, and assuming there was nothing broken or no internal injuries, he could somehow . . . please, God! . . . keep her hidden for a day or two until he somehow located a women's resource center or whatever the hell you called those places that would find her a safe house.

Yeah, there were a lot of "somehows" involved, but nothing he couldn't handle.

*Easy Peasy!* he thought.

Then, *Easy Peasy shit!* as his plans ran smack-dab into the first roadblock.

There was a long-haul, flatbed truck parked in front of the castle. Exiting from the driver's side was none other than Vikar, who'd had no trouble maneuvering a long-ship on the high seas at one time but knew diddly-squat about motor vehicles, as evidenced by the many dings on every car he owned.

Armod climbed out of the passenger side. Svein and Jogeir crawled out, too. All four of them must have been sitting on the front bench seat. Talk about cozy!

Then Karl noticed something else. They were carrying axes. Armod, a regular woodsman kind that was used to chop kindling, but the other men had long-handled weapons with pikes on one end and sharp axes on the other, the kind Vikings and medieval knights took into battle.

Through the open double front doors of the castle streamed Alex, about a dozen vangels, and the two children, who had been bundled up in matching blue and pink snowsuits so that they resembled fat, midget snowmen.

Fortunately, the snow was still coming down heavily, covering the windows of his pickup no sooner than the wipers made a pass. Fortunate because that meant that no one could see Faith, who still slept soundly. He was beginning to think it was an unnatural sleep.

As quietly as he could, he opened the driver's door, slid out, and carefully shut and locked the vehicle behind him. He shivered at the blast of cold air that hit him after being in the warm truck and wandered over to the big flatbed.

Now that he got closer, he saw the huge . . . *and I mean HUGE* . . . evergreen tree lying in the back, anchored down with many, many bungee cords. They must have bought out the entire supply of the stretchy straps at Walmart.

"Are you crazy?" Alex was yelling at Vikar. "I told you to get a Christmas tree. This is a . . . a forest."

"No, sweetling. You told me to get a *big* Christmas tree. Which I did." He grinned with pleasure and did a little twirl with his battle-axe that caused the children to jump up and down and giggle. Well, as much as they could jump with all that padding.

"Vikar!" she said, folding her arms over the chest of her hoodie. "That tree must be fifty feet tall. The front living room ceiling is thirty feet tall."

"Oh." At first, Vikar seemed surprised, but then he grinned again. "No problem, sweetling. We will just chop it down to size."

Armod, Svein, and Jogeir grinned, too. Apparently, they were having a great time, playing with their axes today. Meanwhile, everyone was being coated with snow.

Alex stepped up closer to the truck. "How many trees did you get, Vikar?"

"Only five. The others are small ones. Only about ten or fifteen feet. While we were out in the forest, we figured you might want more than one, and why waste time making an extra trip. Don't I deserve a kiss *or something* for all my good work, sweetling?" Vikar waggled his snowy eyebrows at his wife.

"Don't you sweetling me," she said, then did in fact lean up and plant a big one on Vikar's smiling lips.

"I'm beginning to like this Christmas celebrating," Vikar said, slapping Alex on the butt when she danced away from him to grab Gunnar, who was attempting to climb up the back of the truck.

Karl figured this was his chance to slip away. As he walked back to his pickup, he heard Gunnora begging her father, "Please, Poppa, make us a snowman. A biiiig one."

"I wanna go sled riding," Gunnar said.

"Yes, yes, yes!" Gunnora agreed. "But first I hafta pee."

Alex groaned.

Climbing back into his pickup, he saw that Faith had awakened and, thankfully, had known to stay put and not make her presence known. She had the passenger window open and was staring outside. Gaping, actually, which was a ludicrous picture, with her swollen lip and one closed eye.

"Oh, my God! It's a palace!" she said with wonder in her voice. Then, she turned to him as he started the engine and began to back up so he could take the alternate driveway around the back. "You live in a palace?"

With the snow covering its bleaker parts, the castle didn't look as run-down and scary as usual. "It's a castle, not a palace."

"Big difference!" she said at his splitting hairs. "Are you a prince or something?"

He had to laugh at that. "Hardly!"

"But this is your home?"

"Well, it's sort of a family residence. I do a lot of traveling." That sounded like more splitting hairs, even to his own ears. But how else could he explain without really explaining vangeldom?

"And all those people out there . . . are they your family?"

"Um. In a way."

"Like a blended family."

*Help me, Lord!* "Sure."

"And they all live here?"

*Them and about thirty others, give or take a hundred or so, on occasion.* "Yep."

"Wow! I always wanted to have a big family."

"You are an only child?"

"I had a brother who was three years older than me, but we were separated when I was only five years old and put in foster care. Separate families. Last I heard, Zach was in prison."

The sadness in her voice told a story he wasn't prepared to hear right now. Especially since he was in the back courtyard. He turned off the truck. Time to put his plan into effect.

"Listen, you stay in the car while I go check on something." He hopped out before she could protest. Popping into the kitchen, he found the coast clear. Lizzie was the only one about, and when she paid no attention to him but went into the large pantry at the other end, he went back outside, leaving the outside door open.

When Faith's sneakers sank ankle deep in the snow, he picked her up, without hesitation, and carried her inside, closing the door with his hip. Lizzie was thankfully still out of sight. Everyone else was probably out front admiring the Christmas trees, or not admiring them but enjoying the spectacle.

Faith was staring googly-eyed . . . a one-eyed google, that is . . . at the immense kitchen. But he had no time to pause for her to get a good look. Quickly, he entered the closed stairway and made his way upward. Her weight was slight and no burden to carry. In fact, he kind of liked the way she wrapped her arms around his neck and laid her face on his shoulder, seeming to trust him.

He heard voices on the second floor, but he didn't pause to see who was about. Instead, he took the remaining steps at warp speed and soon entered his bedroom at this end of the wide hallway on the third floor. Setting Faith on her feet, he said in a teasing note that came from God only knew where, "Honey, we're home."

She turned in a slow circle, soaking everything in.

The room wasn't small . . . none of them were in this castle. About twenty by thirty. It had a double bed with one of Alex's many quilt purchases on it. This one was vividly colored in a pattern she'd told him was called God's Pinwheel. There was a desk, a bureau, a small, flat-screen TV in a sitting area with a fat, upholstered chair with a floor lamp next to it for reading, two large, many-paned windows, one of which had a padded seat in front of it. The walls were plain white plaster, and the only thing adorning them was a crucifix above the bed and on the other side, a framed print of a summer landscape . . . a farm, ironically. That's probably why he had picked this particular room.

The furnishings weren't historically correct for a hundred-year-old castle, but Alex had enough to do restoring the first floor to the way it had been. Comfort was the key in the bedrooms. Thus far.

"This is beautiful," Faith said on a sigh, taking off her hat, and scarf, and coat.

Her expectations must be low for her to consider this beautiful. *Adequate* would be a better description.

She shivered suddenly, although it was fairly warm in the room, a new heating system having been installed in the castle several months ago. For a small fortune, Vikar was quick to tell one and all. You could heat a small village for the same amount, Vikar contended.

But her shivering recalled to Karl that he needed to tend to Faith's injuries, whatever they might be.

"There's a bathroom across the hall," he told her.

She nodded, but didn't seem to be in need of the facilities at the moment. She was checking out the paperback novels arranged between two bookends on the desk. Mostly thrillers.

This was awkward.

"Faith, I need to examine you for . . . injuries."

That caught her attention. "Are you a doctor?"

"No, but I have some medical training." He'd been a medic at one point, as well as a sniper, in the Army.

And he'd served as an aide to Sigurd on some missions. Sigurd, one of the seven Sigurdsson brothers, was in fact a physician.

"I think I'm all right. I'd just like to lie down for a while if you don't mind."

"That's a good idea. You lie down, let me assess your condition, then you can take a nap."

"No way am I lying on that pretty quilt with these dirty clothes."

"Huh?" She didn't look dirty to him. In fact, her sweatshirt and jeans looked old and faded but clean.

"I was scrubbing the bathroom floor when you arrived," she confessed, her face turning pink, as if that was something to be embarrassed about. She put a hand to her flat stomach, a gesture that he'd noticed she did a lot.

"Did that bastard kick you in the stomach or punch you there?" he snarled.

His rough voice startled her, he could tell, and he told himself to be extra careful with her in future. He didn't want her to think she'd picked up another violent man. Not that Karl wasn't violent when need be. But not with women. Unless they were Lucies.

"No. Not this time," she told him, sitting down on the edge of the old upholstered chair he'd rescued from the Dumpster when Alex was spring-cleaning one of the attics. No worry about getting that thing dirty!

Faith began to toe off her sneakers, then curl her toes in their pink socks into the soft, braided rug on the floor. His cue to leave, he guessed.

"Uh, I'll go get your suitcase, and you can change

your clothes if you want," he said though he didn't give a rat's ass about dirt on the damn quilt, "then we'll see what we can do about those bruises on your face . . . and, uh, anywhere else."

She nodded, then started to yawn widely but stopped when her split lip began to bleed again.

He handed her a tissue from the box on his desk, and she dabbed at the moisture.

"I still think you should go to the ER."

"No! I just need to rest, then I'll get out of your way." Under her breath, she added, "Somehow."

"You're not in my way," he said, which was an out-and-out lie, which they both recognized.

She arched her brows at him in teasing disbelief, then had to hold the tissue against her mouth when another yawn reflex hit her.

Karl was beginning to be concerned about her need to sleep. She'd already slept almost an hour in the pickup truck on the way here; he had to wonder if she was in shock or something.

"Are you hungry?"

"Not really. I'm more tired at the moment."

He got the message and left, closing the door behind him.

After parking his truck in the underground garage, he snuck Faith's suitcase upstairs. When he got there, she was already in his bed, the quilt pulled up to her neck. On a nearby chair, she'd folded her jeans and T-shirt, along with the pink hat and scarf. Her jacket hung in the open closet.

He set the suitcase down and, without hesitation,

lifted the quilt. Her skinny body was covered only with a plain white bra and panties and the pink socks. Everywhere he looked, he saw new and old bruises, including her ribs. And then there were the two old scars of raised flesh on her thigh, the letters L and B that Jeanette had told Karl were carved there by the abuser.

The fact that her eyelids did not even flutter as he looked at her near-nude body alarmed him as much as her injuries.

Leroy Brown was going to pay for this, sure as Karl was a vampire angel, but for now his biggest concern was Faith. Karl was no fool. He knew when he needed help.

He found Alex down in the main salon, or what they called the front living room, directing the moving of furniture to accommodate the big-ass tree that six vangels were hauling in.

Tapping her on the shoulder, Karl said, "Alex, I need a favor."

She had been laughing at something one of the children said and turned to him with a smile, which immediately disappeared on seeing the expression on his face. "What?"

"I need you to come upstairs with me."

"What is it, Karl?"

"Um, something personal."

"Can it wait 'til later?"

"No, it can't wait."

"Perhaps Svein or Jogeir could help you."

"I have a problem that requires a woman's hand," he said with exasperation.

"Okaaay," she said, calling out to Armod to keep an eye on the twins.

As they went side by side up the wide, front stairway, he tried to prepare her. "There's someone in my bedroom. She's in pretty bad shape."

"She? What have you done, Karl?" She stopped at the first landing, hands on hips, and scowled at him.

"It's not what I've done. Well, it is what I've done since I brought her here, but her condition was caused by her boyfriend. Who is no longer her boyfriend if I have any say in the matter."

"She who?"

"Faith Larson."

"Do you have a relationship with this woman?"

"Hell, no! I mean, I hardly know her. She's a waitress at the diner out on Route 322."

"Let me see if I understand. There's a woman you ran into in a diner who was being abused in some way in a public place. So, instead of calling the police, you brought her here."

"No!" He combed his hands in frustration through the short bristles of his hair. "I went to her trailer. Leroy wasn't there until we were leaving."

"Leroy?"

"Leroy Brown, the douche-bag boyfriend. And, yes, Leroy Brown, like the junkyard-dog song."

A sudden thought seemed to occur to Alex. "Is he a Lucie?"

"No, but he could be. He reeked of lemony evil." To

vangels, humans who were evil or about to commit some great evil exuded the citrusy scent of lemons.

"Did you kill him? You know how Vikar feels about calling attention to us here at the castle."

"No, but I temporarily incapacitated him."

"How did—"

"Never mind all that. I'll explain later." They continued up the next flight of stairs. "One more thing, Alex, please don't tell Vikar about Faith's being here."

She didn't like that idea, at all, he could tell.

"Maybe you could just not mention that I brought an outsider here unless he asks."

"I don't know—"

"She'll be gone before he even realizes she's been here."

"I don't like secrets." Worry creased her brow, but she didn't chastise him any longer or plague him with more questions as they walked down the long hall.

All bets were off, though, when they entered the bedroom.

Whether she slept soundly or was unconscious, Faith never awakened. Not even when Karl uncovered her again.

Alex gasped as she viewed Faith's injuries, as well as the carved initials on her thigh, but she made a sound of real distress when she put a hand to the young woman's forehead and proclaimed, "Fever! Get cold washcloths right away, then we need to get her to a hospital."

"No! I promised her there would be no hospital." When he returned with several cold cloths and watched as she placed a folded one over Faith's forehead, he asked, "Can't we take care of her ourselves?"

"I don't see how." She paused, and said, "Get a glass of water and a couple of Tylenol. Then, you better go tell Vikar to call Sigurd."

*Tell Vikar?* Karl groaned, but he knew that Alex was right. This situation had escalated beyond his control. Still, he muttered, "Vikar is going to kill me. Or worse yet, he'll tell Mike."

"No, he's not, Karl. You probably saved this woman's life by taking her away from that evil man."

Karl felt a little better.

But not much.

"You can also tell Vikar I said that he's not allowed to yell at you," she added.

"Oh, that'll help. He'll just give me one of those black looks that are even worse than his roar."

"His roars are just loud meows. He's a pussycat, at heart."

"Who's a pussycat?" a loud male voice said with mock chagrin from the open doorway, immediately followed by, "What the hell?" as new eyes took in the scene in the bedroom.

And, yes, it was a roar.

## Chapter 4

**And then the other shoe dropped . . .**

SIGURD ARRIVED WITH his leather doctor's bag at about seven and went immediately upstairs to examine Faith. By then, via the vangel grapevine, which was more effective than a bullhorn, everyone in the castle knew what Karl had done.

Not long after, Karl got himself booted out of his own bedroom by making a nuisance of himself with all his questions and second-guessing and the occasional cussword. Instead, Alex offered to stay and help her brother-in-law physician, along with one of the female vangels who assisted Lizzie in the kitchen. It was just as well. Karl had trouble breathing when he heard Sigurd remark on the various injuries.

"Looks like the bastard kicked her in the ribs with a steel-toed shoe."

"The bum must wear a ring. When he slapped her, the metal scraped a gouge in her cheek."

"One of her teeth appears to be loose."

"Do you see how crooked that little finger is?"

It was enough to make a grown man weep!

Vikar got the boot, too. He said, "Mike is going to have an angel fit," way too many times. Alex ordered her grumbling husband to put their children to bed. If he knew the usual pattern, Karl guessed that Vikar would fall asleep, too. The two rascals had a way of wearing a person down. Which was just as well; Karl didn't need to hear any more pronouncements of how much trouble he was in.

Heading toward the electronics room, which had been set up by Harek, one of the seven brothers, who was a computer genius, Karl decided to put his free time to good use. Booting up one of the simplest of the PCs, he googled, "Women's Shelters" within a fifty-mile radius of the castle's zip code. There were fifty. Pulling out his cell phone, he began to dial.

After fifteen minutes, he hung up in the middle of yet another call. They wanted to know his name, telephone number, address, practically everything including his criminal record, as if he were the abuser.

"All I want to know is what measures you take to protect a woman's identity if she gets dropped off there," he'd finally yelled at one young woman, who sounded bored as she asked questions from a crib sheet.

"Dropped off?" she asked with sudden alertness. "You would need to bring the woman inside, sir."

*Yeah, right. So the cops could arrest me.*

He knew there were good people, volunteers mostly, at these shelters and that he was handling this all wrong, mainly because he was trying to be secretive when that raised red flags of suspicion. He needed to go about this in another way. Maybe if a woman made the calls . . .

He went out into the hall and saw Regina approaching. Not his first choice under any circumstances. Regina had been a witch back in the 1200s, a real, cauldron-brewing, broom-riding practitioner of the black arts. Regina was always threatening to put curses on the male parts of the vangels who annoyed her. Karl had always wondered if she might have been a lesbian, not that the word was used then, but she was probably just an unpleasant, male-hating female. She wasn't that nice to her fellow females, either, come to think of it.

"Hey, Regina," he said with as much warmth as he could muster. "Would you mind doing me a favor?"

"Drop dead, lackwit," she said, swanning by. The black cat riding on her shoulder hissed at him, too.

So much for *that* woman helping him.

He walked down to the kitchen. Maybe Lizzie would be more amenable.

The kitchen smelled wonderful. Lizzie and two of her vangel helpers, the sisters Esther and Hester, were baking cookies. Dozens and dozens of cookies.

Lizzie wore her usual Victorian, upper-class attire. White, high-necked, lace-trimmed blouse, tucked into a full-length black skirt. Over that, a long white apron. Her gray-threaded brown hair was tucked in a bun on top of her head. She was whacking walnuts on a cutting board with the flat side of her meat cleaver. Whack, whack, whack! Shells were flying everywhere. Every time she whacked, Esther and Hester jumped and scurried to pick up loose shells.

"Um, what are you doing?" Karl asked.

"Shelling walnuts." Whack, whack, whack! "For the bloody damn fruitcakes I'm making." Whack, whack, whack! "What does it look like I'm doing?" she sniped.

*Oh, Lord! Another sourpuss!* "Wouldn't it be easier to use a nutcracker?"

"Hmpfh! This way I get to release my temper." Whack, whack, whack! "On nuts, instead of someone's head." She looked pointedly at his head. Whack, whack, whack!

*Maybe Lizzie isn't be the best person to make calls on Faith's behalf.* "Hey! I didn't do anything."

"Yet." She glared at him for a moment, then remarked, "You look paler than a ghost." Whack, whack, whack!

When vangels went too long without killing Lucies or saving sinners, their skin got paler and paler. He wasn't sure if that was the reason for his pallor or the shock of the situation he found himself in. Either way, he went over to the commercial-size fridge and took out a carton of Fake-O, the synthetic blood that provided a temporary fix for vangels. He took a long swig and grimaced. Fake-O tasted like curdled cat piss.

In an emergency, vangels could also take small amounts of blood from ceorl vangels, like Esther and Hester, which was equally distasteful to Karl. He really felt like a vampire then, which he was, of course, but he liked to think he was more angel than vampire.

*What a crock!* Karl thought at his mental rationalization. "What is this?" he asked then, grabbing a warm cookie out of one of the plastic storage bins lined up along the counter. "Wow! It's really good."

"Snickerdoodles," Lizzie grumbled. Whack, whack, whack! "And don't you dare snicker. Look at this." She shoved a piece of flour-smudged notebook paper at Karl. "The Missus expects me to make ten dozen of each of these cookies for Christmas."

He did, in fact, have trouble stifling a snicker as he read the list. Fruitcake, snickerdoodles, gingerbread men (and women), chocolate chip cookies, decorated, cut-out sugar cookies, snowballs, shortbread, rum balls, sand tarts, thumbprint cookies, and macaroons. "Um. That's a lot of cookies."

"I told her to just buy out all the Keebler cookies in the supermarket, and she said it wouldn't be the same thing. Hah! The vangels here could live on those stupid Oreos." Whack, whack, whack!

"I'm sure if you asked Alex for help, she would assign more vangels here."

Lizzie slammed her cleaver into the cutting board. Luckily, it was a really thick cutting board. Putting her floury hands on both hips, she gave him the evil eye, probably learned from Regina. "Are you insinuating that I can't run my own kitchen?"

"No, no, no! I just meant . . ." Oh, this was a losing battle. He glanced at his wristwatch. "Look at the time. I need to go . . . do something."

As he left the kitchen, he heard Lizzie telling Ester and Hester, "If any of them vangels refuse to eat my fruitcake after all this trouble, I'll personally shove it down their barmy throats. With the wooden end of my axe. They think I got rid of my axe, but I save it for special occasions. Hee, hee, hee." Whack, whack, whack!

Karl escaped to the front living room, where he pulled a wingback chair up closer to the hearth fire so that he could prop his feet on the brass fender. Even though there were other vangels in the large room, which was now dominated by the enormous blue spruce tree, everyone was somewhat quiet, except for the occasional laugh, or grunt, or yawn. And the Christmas music, which had been playing nonstop ever since the word escaped that the castle would be getting in the holiday spirit. Luckily, someone had turned down the volume on the sound system so that Nat King Cole's crooning about chestnuts on an open fire was only a minor distraction in the background. While the kids had been awake, the song du jour had been by Alvin and the Chipmunks. At one point, Vikar had threatened to wrap a hula hoop around Armod's neck for introducing the little ones to what had to be the world's most irritating singing group.

He considered asking some of the vangels in the room for help, or at least advice, on getting rid of Faith . . . rather, finding a safe place for the poor woman, other than the castle. But then he decided to wait and discuss the situation with Alex.

Jogeir and Svein were playing a game of chess before one of the wide bay windows. Even from here, Karl could see that snow continued to come down in flakes the size of golf balls. Twenty inches were expected to accumulate by morning.

Tofa, a fine artist, was touching up one of her wall murals, which had been scratched when they brought in the tree. She was not a happy camper.

Moddam, who had been one of the stoneworkers on the Roman Coliseum, was fast asleep in one of the more comfortable upholstered chairs, his arms folded over his burly chest, his booted feet resting on a hassock. The poor man did hard labor, day after day, trying to restore the stonework on this crumbling castle.

Bodil, a former slave in the Byzantine emperor's Imperial Gardens, knelt before a low coffee table, where she was arranging pine boughs with holly berries and a red bow into a massive wreath to be hung on the front door. She'd already made about fifty feet of garlands to be hung in swags, whatever the hell swags were, along the staircase.

For more than an hour, Karl just sat. He'd never felt more like having a smoke, but he was determined to stay off the cigarettes. Not that he was concerned about dying from the nicotine, a morbid joke if there ever was one, but it was a filthy habit. Enough about his addiction!

If it weren't for his worry over Faith, Karl would have found the fresh pine scent, the warm fire, the soft music, and the unusual quiet . . . unusual for vangels, that is . . . to be soothing. As it was, he couldn't relax with all the questions hammering in his head.

Finally, Sigurd came up and dropped his bag to the floor with a long sigh of exhaustion. Tugging another wingback chair closer to the fire, Sigurd plopped down in it and leaned back, closing his eyes for a few moments. "That feels so good!"

With his long blond ponytail and day-old whiskers, he didn't look like any doctors Karl had ever known, but word was that Sigurd had a great reputation at Johns Hopkins Hospital, where he worked, when he was not off on vangel missions.

Karl was almost afraid to ask about Faith's condition. Instead, he said, "Thanks for coming tonight, Sig."

"No problem," Sigurd replied, eyes still closed. When he opened them, he stared at Karl through eyes that were the same as all the vangels, clear blue, sometimes morphing to silver-gray when in some high emotion. "Faith is going to be all right, Karl, provided she gets rest and food and a little TLC, none of which she appears to have had for some time now. And provided she doesn't go back to her abuser, of course."

"I'll make sure she doesn't go back." The anger that had been boiling in Karl all day simmered to the surface again.

Sigurd shrugged. "It wouldn't be the first time a victim returned to her partner. Codependency is a symptom of abused women. You don't have to be a psychiatrist, or a physician, to see that this isn't the first beating Faith has had."

"I'll make sure she doesn't go back," Karl repeated. "How bad off is she?"

"Some cracked ribs, which are very painful but should heal on their own, in time. I've given her some painkillers and left more behind to be taken, as needed. That should help her to sleep through the night." Sigurd made a sound of disgust, and remarked, "You know about the initials carved on her thigh?"

Karl nodded.

"What kind of man does that to a woman?" Sigurd asked. "Never mind. You and I both know about the evil in this world. You're right, though. You can't let her go back to him."

"Is Alex still up there?"

"Yeah. Someone should stay with Faith through the night, just to make sure she's all right. If nothing else, she shouldn't wake alone, in a strange place."

"I'll stay with her," Karl offered. "Alex needs to get some sleep herself."

"You might want to get one of the women to take over for Alex. From what Alex says about Vikar, you're already on my big brother's shit list for bringing Faith here." Sigurd grinned. They all knew about Vikar's temper, which was bound to be edgier than usual with all the Christmas hoopla. "Man, how did you get involved in this mess?"

Karl was getting tired of having to explain himself, and so his tone was a mite surly when he started to ask, "What else could I—"

Sigurd put his hands up in mock surrender. "Hey, I'm not criticizing. I'm just saying."

"We'll see about who stays with Faith through the night," Karl conceded, but he didn't really mean it. *I am for damn sure going to be the one sitting with Faith tonight. I brought her here. She's my responsibility.* "Are you going back to Baltimore tonight? That blizzard is going to be a bitch for driving."

"I need to be there for a morning consult, but I won't be driving."

Karl realized then that Sigurd must have teletransported here. It was a talent that most vangels had, to be used only in rare emergencies. Too much, and they might call unwanted attention to themselves in all their various outside jobs.

"There's one more thing, Karl."

Uh-oh! He didn't like the sound of Sigurd's voice.

"Faith thinks she might be pregnant."

Karl's wildly beating heart suddenly went thunk. What next? Could this situation get any more complicated? "Oh, fuck!" he exclaimed. Vangels tried not to use sacrilegious swear words, but sometimes foul language escaped nonetheless. "Fuck!" was okay, "Jesus Christ!" was not. Well, maybe not okay, but not as bad.

*My brain is melting here with all this stress.*
*Since when do I get stressed out by little things?*
*A baby is not a little thing!*

"You said *might* be pregnant," Karl said hopefully.

"Yeah. If she is, it's only about one month."

"Couldn't you do a test or something?"

"I didn't happen to bring one of those little sticks with me," Sigurd said sarcastically. "I'm not an obstetrician. And don't even think of going out to some drugstore tonight. Like you said, driving's already hazardous, and I doubt Mike would consider a pregnancy test enough of an emergency to teletransport."

Karl groaned at the mention of Mike. He had been hoping . . . he still was . . . that their archangel mentor wouldn't have to find out about his bringing a human into their midst.

That hope was shot dead in its tracks when Sigurd stood and stretched before picking up his bag, and said, "Speaking of Mike. Vikar got a message that there will be a meeting of the VIK here at the castle a week from now. Something about some new trouble brewing from Jasper."

The VIK was the ruling council of all the vangels, comprised of the seven Sigurdsson brothers. Vikar, Trond, Ivak, Mordr, Sigurd, Cnut, and Harek.

"A new mission?" Karl guessed.

"Sounds like," Sigurd agreed.

That's all they needed. The vangel holiday madness that Alex was no doubt planning on top of St. Michael the

Archangel arriving on the scene, not to mention Faith up in Karl's bedroom, and Karl possibly having to leave on some Lucie mission.

Karl held Sigurd's gaze for a long moment. The unanswered question was: Would Faith be gone by then?

And where would she go?

And why did he suddenly care so much?

---

## Chapter 5

---

*It's beginning to look a lot like . . .
vampires? . . .*

AFTER TWO DAYS confined to Karl's third-floor bedroom, Faith was bored. Still sore, of course. What else was new? And so weak that when she got up to use the bathroom, which was just across the hall, it felt like a marathon to her wobbly legs.

All she did was eat and sleep and watch TV, mostly reality shows that were downright depressing. She had enough reality in her own life . . . and depression.

More than anything, she was itching to explore the castle while it was still her temporary abode. God only knew how much longer she would be permitted to stay. Karl was searching desperately for some women's resource place that would find her a safe home. And while

Alex and Vikar were not rude to her, they were clearly worried about her meeting the other people who lived in the castle. Why, she wasn't sure. It was almost as if they were some weird cult that lived here secretly. As if Faith cared!

No one had actually said the words, that her welcome was a short-lived one, but Faith sensed it in the way they pushed for her speedy recovery. In fact, Karl had told her that he would get her car and have it ready to go whenever she was ready

Faith appreciated Karl's efforts to find her a safe haven, but she had no intention of leaving her future in anyone else's hands. She'd done that for too long. Now that she had escaped Leroy, for good, she planned to "disappear." Once she was a little bit stronger. Maybe next week.

There was one thing that held her back, and it wasn't the growing affection she felt for the sweet young man who'd saved her. No, it was another "person" all together. She put her hand to her belly. If she was pregnant . . . well, that would create a whole new obstacle for her plans. Not that she considered a baby an obstacle. A complication, that was all.

"Are you talkin' to yourself?" a small voice asked. "I talk to myself when I hafta do quiet time."

Faith jerked around from where she was standing by the window, looking out over the snowy terrain. Dizziness swept over her at the quick movement, and she had to hold on to the back of a chair to keep from toppling over.

A child was peeking through the partially open doorway. No, it was two children. Blond-haired twins, by the similar looks and size of them. A boy and a girl. About three years old and adorable. Wearing matching denim coveralls over long-sleeved white T-shirts with blinking-light, neon-colored athletic shoes on their little feet.

"Maybe she's talkin' to us, Nora," the boy said to the girl.

"Maybe. That means we hafta go in, Gun. To be polite," the girl replied. "We wouldn't be botherin' her then."

"Nope. We gotta go in." The boy looked at Faith, hopefully. "Do you want us to come in?"

"Sure," she said, glad for the company.

The two little scamps rushed in, causing the door to swing inward and slam against the wall.

"Hullo! My name is Gunnora, but you can call me Nora," the little girl said. "I brought these for your owies." She handed Faith a half dozen Winnie the Pooh Band-Aids. "Momma said you're sick in bed from all your owies, and we shouldn't bother you."

"I'm Gunnar, but everyone calls me Gun. Like a weapon. Bang, bang! I brought you these." The boy shoved some lollipops at her. "When I'm sick, lollipops taste good."

"Thank you so much," Faith said, placing her "gifts" on the dresser. "Would you like to sit down?"

Before the words were out of her mouth, the boy was on the bed, bouncing up and down, and the girl was crawling up onto the edge of the chair, her little legs hanging only halfway to the floor.

"I doan think you look like you been through a meat grinder," Gunnar said. "Thass what Poppa tol' Lizzie."

"That was not nice, Gun," Nora admonished her brother, then turned to Faith. "Do they hurt?"

"Not so much anymore," Faith said, putting her hand to her face, where her lip had healed but was still puffy, and her eye had finally healed enough that she could open it. She must look awful to the little kids, though.

"The vangels look worser than that when they come back from missions sometimes. They even bleed when they get stabbed," Gunnar told her.

Faith had a hard time thinking of a little boy by the nickname *Gun*. It might just as well be *Rifle* or *Pistol*.

"Vangels?" Faith asked. *Stabbed?* She was right. They were some kind of cult or something. Or a gang. Like Hell's Angels. Maybe even the mob. Did the Mafia exist in Pennsylvania?

Nora nodded. "Everyone here is a vangel, 'cept for me and Gun, and Momma."

"And Aunt Nicole and Aunt Gabby and baby Michael and Aunt Miranda and their kids when they come to visit," Gunnar added.

"Yep," Nora agreed.

Faith decided to ask Karl about it later. It probably wasn't wise to pump the children for information.

"Can we watch television?" Nora asked. "We're allowed to watch cartoons. As much as we want. Even at nighttime." The little scamp was clearly lying.

Gunnar's head shot up with interest, and he was off the bed in a flash, crawling up on the big chair to sit next to his sister. When they shifted their little butts back, their legs didn't even hang over the cushion.

"How old are you two?"

"Three," Gunnar said.

"Almost," Nora added.

"Where are your Momma and Poppa?" Faith asked while she flicked through the channels.

"Poppa made Karl drive Momma to the mall to buy Christmas decorations. Karl didn't wanna go to any blasted mall with all the crowds and noise, but he's in trouble, so he had to go. Poppa said so," Nora told her. "We wanted to go, but we're in trouble, too, because we played songs by Alvin and the Chipmunks too many times and gave Poppa a headache."

"And where is your poppa now?"

"Poppa is watchin' us so Momma can shop 'til she drops, but he had to go down to the dungeon for a minute to help the vangels sword fighting, and he tol' us to stay put or die. He was just kiddin'," Gunnar contributed.

"Have you ever been to this . . . um, dungeon?"

"Uh-huh," Nora said. "It's where most of the vangels sleep."

Oh, Lord! This just gets worse and worse. "What exactly are vangels?" she asked before she could stop herself.

"Viking vampire angels," the two children said, as if that were an everyday normal thing for someone to be.

"Poppa says you're prob'ly a Viking, too."

"Me? Why? Do I look like a Viking?"

" 'Cause of your name," Nora said with a giggle.

"Faith? My name Faith makes me a Viking."

"Your other name," Gunnar explained. "Larson. In the long-ago time, when Poppa was a boy, it meant son of Lars. Just like Poppa is Vikar Sigurdsson, or Vikar, son of Sigurd."

Faith had no idea if she had Norse blood in her veins or not. Her father had skipped town when she was five, not much older than these kids here, and her brother Zach had been eight. Their mother had apparently just been diagnosed with cancer. When she died soon after, Faith and Zach been sent to different foster homes.

The twins were apparently bored with the chitchat by now. Their eyes kept darting to the TV set.

Faith soon found the Nickelodeon Channel for them. A short time later, they sat with their eyes glued to the screen, lollipops in their mouths, when an adult voice could be heard yelling, "Gunnar! Gunnora! Where are you? I'm going to paddle your little arses if you don't come out. Right now!"

"Uh-oh!" Gunnar and Gunnora said as one. Looking at each other with some silent message, they jumped off the chair and scooted behind it.

Soon Vikar loomed in the doorway. He was wearing slim black pants and hiking-style boots, no shirt. Perspiration beaded his chest and forehead, as if he'd been engaged in some strenuous activity. In one of his hands, he carried a huge sword.

"You wouldn't? Surely, you wouldn't strike a child with that?" Faith said indignantly.

"Huh?" Vikar said. Then he realized what Faith meant and grinned. "No, I wouldn't use my sword on a child. Or my hand." His quick glance around the room took in the cartoons on the television, the lollipop sticking to the arm of the chair, and the Winnie the Pooh Band-Aids on the dresser. With a slow drawl, he added, "But I might have to cancel Christmas if two naughty children continue to misbehave."

"Poppa! You can't!" Nora exclaimed, darting around the chair.

"Santa has to come. He has to," Gunnar added. "I already sent my list."

"You mean that three-page greedy treatise?" Vikar inquired, leaning on his sword, the tip of which was buried in the hooked rug.

His sarcasm passed over the boy, who corrected, "It was four pages."

Vikar rolled his eyes and pointed to the open doorway. "Out! Your mother will be back any minute, and she will blame me if you are not in your bedroom practicing your numbers."

The two munchkins ran out the door and could be heard clomping down the steps, laughing and shouting the whole way.

"I hope Momma remembered the candy canes. I'm gonna eat ten of them," Nora said.

"I'm gonna eat so many, I'm gonna puke," Gunnar countered, as if that were something to be desired.

When they were alone, Vikar said, "Sorry I am that my children bothered you."

"Don't apologize. They were no bother at all. And, please, don't punish them for coming up here. They were a welcome distraction."

Just then, from a distance, they heard the blare of a car horn, or maybe a truck horn, and a commotion of shouts and running feet down below.

"That would be my wife returning from her shopping spree. I must go help unload her purchases," he said. "Why don't you take a nap? Or something?"

When he was gone, Faith thought. *A nap? Again? I don't think so!* She made her way carefully across the room and through the door, down the corridor toward the front of the castle, where she could hear the sounds of many voices on the lower level. Her ribs hurt more than anything, but she hated taking so many of the pain pills because, frankly, they made her sleep even more.

Most of the bedrooms and the hallway on this third floor were furnished in the same no-frills way as Karl's, but when she got to the second floor, she saw evidence of restoration in progress. Ornate mirrors over heavy, antique-looking tables. Gilt-framed paintings. No portraits, she noticed, but lots of landscapes or pictures loaded with Cupids. In some of the bedrooms, she could see heavily carved, high-posted bed frames with matching furniture from about a hundred years or so ago, which was the age of the castle, according to Karl.

When she got to the top of what became a wide staircase leading down to the first floor . . . so wide it would fit in some grand hotel . . . she stopped and leaned on the banister. From this second-floor landing, she could see a lot, and, besides, she was winded already.

People were laughing and chattering as they came

in carrying boxes and shopping bags with logos from Macy's, Home Depot, Walmart, Best Buy, Target, and Interior Décor. One of the people even wore a Santa hat, it was Alex. Elvis was crooning "Blue Christmas" from somewhere. And the smell of evergreen filled the air. Probably the tree she'd seen on the flatbed truck the day they'd arrived. The children were so excited, they kept jumping up and down and clapping their hands with delight. In the midst of it all, she saw Karl, whose face was half-hidden by the tall box he held in both hands.

She eased halfway down the staircase and sat on a step, still unnoticed by those below. There were about two dozen adults, mostly men, and the two children, who'd moved into the room where the giant Christmas tree held center stage. Unadorned, but beautiful.

Alex was displaying some of her purchases. Lights, ornaments, tinsel, a star. Each one drew oohs and aahs. Meanwhile, a young woman came in with a tray carrying an assortment of cookies, while another young woman brought in a tray of hot chocolate . . . Faith could tell by the rich smell that wafted up to her . . . and what someone said with a groan was something called "Fake-O." Faith recognized the two young women as Ester and Hester, who sometimes brought meals to her bedroom.

Faith realized in that moment that this was the kind of holiday home she'd always dreamed about. Oh, not a castle. Her dreams were never that lofty. But a large family full of Christmas cheer, safe in the love that surrounded them, that was the ultimate fantasy to her. Foster homes, at least the many she'd resided in, had never provided this sense of belonging. In fact, she'd always felt like an outsider, even when there had been large families.

Suddenly, Faith noticed something else. Every single person, except for Alex and the two children, had pointy incisors. In fact, on some of them they appeared to be actual fangs. She frowned as she tried to concentrate. What had the twins told her about almost everyone in the castle being vangels? Viking *vampire* angels? She didn't see any evidence of wings, but fangs. Oh, yeah!

Had she landed in a vampire enclave or nest or cult or whatever you called it? Like that *True Blood* or *Twilight*? She knew that the town of Transylvania was kind of crazy with all the Dracula nonsense, but this was different. Was it possible? For some reason, she wasn't frightened, just puzzled.

Just then, Karl glanced up and noticed her staring at them. He quickly looked around and must have seen what she'd seen. The fangs. Turning back to her, he shrugged, as if to say, "Now you know."

He came up, two steps at a time, and sat down beside her, placing the box in front of them, down two steps. "I bought this for you," he said.

"For me? A present?"

"No big deal. Just a little prelit Christmas tree for your room. I know how confined you've been feeling. It has tiny pink poinsettias on it, and I thought since you like pink so much . . . oh, shit! What did I say wrong?"

Faith was weeping, big tears streaming down her face.

She couldn't help herself. It had been so long since a man had treated her so nicely with no ulterior motive. "Nothing is wrong. Thank you, thank you!" Without thinking, she pulled his face down to hers and kissed him. His lips were cool from just coming in from outside.

He was momentarily shocked by her gesture, she could tell, but then he kissed her back, cupping her face with his cold hands. It was a gentle kiss to accommodate her still-swollen lip, but it was erotic nonetheless, with tendrils of sensation snaking out to other parts of her body. Somehow, she was on his lap, her arms wrapped around his neck, and his hands were caressing her back and thigh and rump, wherever he could reach. His lips and fingers were no longer cold, but hot, hot, hot, and they were melting her. His tongue was in her mouth, and he tasted of peppermint. *Candy canes, no doubt.* Santa's elves supposedly handed them out at the mall. But, oh, she was developing a taste for peppermint kisses.

Just then, the sound of clapping crept into her dazed senses.

Karl drew away from her and blinked. He was as testosterone buzzed as she was in hormone-humming mode. She could see it in his silvery blue eyes.

The two of them turned as one to look at the crowded hall, where everywhere was clapping at the spectacle they had just put on. Faith felt her face heat with embarrassment. What had come over her?

She saw at a glance that Karl was blushing, too.

The only one not clapping was Vikar, who tossed his

hands out in surrender, and said, "You might as well come down. The cat's out of the bag now."

"What cat, Poppa?" Nora asked.

"What bag, Poppa?" Gunnar asked. "Oooh, did Santa bring us a kitty?"

"Santa doesn't come until Christmas Eve, silly. Poppa must mean Regina's cat," Nora told her brother.

Karl stood and helped Faith to her feet. "I suppose you expect me to apologize for that kiss," he said.

She shook her head. "I'm the one who kissed you."

He arched his brows as if that was debatable. "It's been forty-two years since I've kissed a woman," he told her then, "and that kiss was hot damn well worth the wait."

Wow! For a man of few words, he sure knew how to charm the pants off a girl. And she meant that literally. More importantly, the cold hard knot that had been lodged deep inside her melted some more.

He winked at her then.

The melting turned into a puddle.

And Faith remembered that there was another part to her Christmas fantasy, and Karl had just fulfilled it.

Love took seed in her heart and began to bloom. It didn't matter that she'd just left another man. It didn't matter that she hardly knew Karl. It didn't matter that she might be pregnant. It didn't matter that she looked like a skinny, beat-up, bag lady, and Karl was a hot hunk. It didn't matter that she was clearly older than he was. It didn't matter that she would be here only a short while.

For now, she was in love. Head over heels, love at almost first sight, with the added bonus that it was Christmastime. The lyrics of that sexy Mariah Carey song, "All I Want For Christmas Is You," suddenly came on the sound system.

And she thought, *Oh, yeah!*

## Chapter 6

*Was it love, or was it lust? Did it matter? . . .*

KARL WAS FALLING in love.

It might have been forty-eight years since he'd first had a crush on Sally Taylor, when they'd both been sophomores at Albert Einstein High School outside Duluth, Minnesota. It had been another three years before they'd gotten married, and they'd had three years of wedded bliss, so to speak, only one of them together, before he got drafted, and then he'd died in Vietnam at age twenty-two. Now, he remained a perpetual twenty-two as a vangel while Sally had gone on to age in normal fashion. She'd died a few years back of cancer. He'd never once stepped out on her, before or since her death, even though he'd never seen her again in all those years. Mike's orders. She'd never remarried, either.

But this was no crush he felt for Faith. Somehow, he'd managed to skip all the steps from first attraction to slam-dunk, I-am-a-dead-duck, putty-in-this-woman's-hands. He wasn't sure when or how it had happened. Probably when he'd stopped for one too many coffees at the diner where she worked. Or when he'd seen her battered face at her trailer. Or when she insisted that she did not take charity and would be out of his hair . . . not that he had much . . . once she was stronger.

And here was the worst part. When Vikar, and Trond, and Ivak, and Wrath had found what they called their lifemates, they said there was a distinctive aura that came off their women like a mist, a pheromone, or whatever you called those sex-lure things. In Faith, her woman-scent was a sweet, light scent, like cotton candy. No kidding. He was getting turned on by friggin' spun sugar.

When he'd asked her a short time ago if she noticed any particular scent coming from him, she said, without hesitation, "Peppermint."

That was just great. Vikar and Trond and Ivak and Wrath and their partners gave got neat man/woman-scents like cloves and honey and pine and ginger. He got candy!

And, by the way, he had not been sucking on a damn candy cane at the mall, as Faith had assumed.

Mike was going to have a fit. First of all, because Karl had brought a human into the castle. Secondly, because he'd dared to fall in love with one. Mike had made it more than clear to the VIK, the seven Sigurdsson broth-ers who were the leaders of all the vangels, that there were to be no more relationships with humans. If Mike felt like that with the esteemed VIK, what hope, then, did a lowly vangel like Karl have? None. Not that he was thinking that far ahead to commitment, or relationship, or, God forbid, marriage. His thinking was centered more like a foot below his belly button, but he knew where that would lead. He was not a casual sex kind of guy. Oh, crap! He had to stop thinking about sex, and Faith, before someone noticed the bulge in his jeans.

He could always say he'd developed a sudden hernia from all that shopping. Like that would work!

The best thing would be for him stay away from Faith. But he couldn't.

He went over to where she was perched in the same wingback chair before the fire where he'd sat the night he brought her back to the castle. Vikar had agreed that she could join the activity downstairs, but Alex had insisted that Faith just watch the decorating frenzy and not exert herself. The big tree in this room was almost done, and some of the vangels had moved on to the ones in the family room and the dormitory TV lounge.

Karl tossed another log on the fire and used a poker to stir the flames. When he leaned against the mantel, he realized that the fire was almost too hot. He looked down at Faith, "Having a good time?"

"Wonderful. Everyone has been so nice to me. I'll never remember all their names."

"I don't remember half of them myself, and I live here."

"Which brings up about fifty questions."

"I figured. Can they wait until after dinner? Lizzie is making her version of Amish chicken and dumplings."

"Sounds delicious. Can I eat down here? Please don't tell me I have to go back to my room yet."

"You don't like my bedroom?" Karl teased and could have kicked himself for the innuendo in his words.

She just smiled, and, man, she had the sweetest smile, now that her lips were almost back to normal. "Is your cook's name really Lizzie Borden?"

He nodded.

"Why would anyone name their child after an axe murderer?"

"Shhh!" he said, putting a forefinger to his lips. "Don't let her hear you say that." When he saw the alarm on her face, he quickly added, "I was kidding. Lizzie is in the kitchen, where she reigns supreme. She doesn't let anyone else take over her duties."

"She sounds nice."

"I wouldn't go that far." *Not even close.* "Truth to tell, honey, Lizzie is the real Lizzie Borden." The honey had just slipped out. Damn!

She frowned. "How is that possible? She would have to be more than a hundred years old, wouldn't she? I mean, I'm not sure when Lizzie Borden was alive, but it was surely a long, long time ago.'

"Yes." He waved a hand dismissively then. "I'll explain everything later."

Just then, someone turned off all the lights in the

room so they could get the full effect of the lit Christmas tree.

There was a communal sigh of appreciation from the vangels still in the room.

"Is the star straight?" Vikar asked from the top of the tall extension ladder.

"Perfect," Alex replied. "Come down from there now before you fall and break your head."

"Will you kiss it better?" Vikar waggled his eyebrows at his wife.

She laughed.

"I'll kiss it better, Poppa," Nora offered.

"I'll give you a hug," Gunnar said. "Hugs are more manly. Uncle Trond said so."

"Uncle Trond is full of . . . feathers," Vikar said, coming down the ladder. "Let's go wash our hands before dinner. Mine are covered with pinesap, and you two look like you've eaten half the candy canes already."

"Is my tongue pink?" Gunnar asked, sticking out his tongue.

"You have sticky stuff on your nose," Nora pointed out.

"So do you."

They both grinned impishly, and said, "Cool!"

When they'd gone, Alex came over and sank down into the other wingback chair.

"The tree is beautiful. In fact, the whole room seems magical," Faith said.

"It does, doesn't it?" Alex agreed. "Well worth all the

trouble I had convincing my husband that we should celebrate the holiday this year. Of course, I never meant to
go to this extreme. A small tree. A wreath. That's as far
as I expected." She shrugged. "Vikings! They never do
things halfway."

Karl was afraid Faith would use Alex's mention of Vikings as an opportunity to start grilling them, but all she
said was, "You didn't celebrate Christmas before?"

"We celebrated Christmas, but in a very subdued sort of
way. More the way it should be, I suppose. Midnight Mass,
a special meal on Christmas Day, a few small gifts. Nothing like the extravaganza this is turning into. But I wanted
to do something more this year, now that the children are
old enough to understand." Alex grinned suddenly. "Who
am I kidding? I love the Christmas season. The trees, the
holly, the mistletoe, the carols, the religious *and* commercial aspects. I even like those awful chipmunks."

"I love Christmas, too," Faith said in a small voice.
"But I never really had that kind of family celebration."

Karl and Alex turned to her, waiting for her to elabo-
rate, but she didn't. The sudden sadness on her face said
it all.

"I got a phone call a little while ago from Father Bernard at St. Vladamir's Church. Vikar is going to have a
bird when he finds out," Alex said to no one in particular.
It was as if she was just speaking her thoughts aloud.

"Um, what's the problem at St. Vlad's?" Father Bernard
had been Bernard Jorgensson at one time, a seventeenth-
century cardinal from Denmark who'd failed to take his

celibacy vows seriously enough. He had sired fifteen children. Enough said! You could say he'd earned his fangs the enjoyable way, and his name, as well.

Drinking the symbolic blood of Christ was an important activity for vangels, with all the obvious parallels to their vampire blood activity, and Father Bernard came often to perform Mass in the castle chapel, whenever he could.

While Karl had been zoning off, Alex had been talking. "It's not just that the choir director had a nervous breakdown, but two of the choir members have adult measles, three have the flu, and two quit because they were tired of singing 'Oh, Holy Night.'"

Karl must have missed the point of Alex's explanation. "So that's why he asked if the castle choir would sing the Midnight Mass this year."

"Oh, crap!"

"There's a castle choir?" Faith asked, duly impressed.

"Not a choir per se, but the men here have marvelous voices."

Faith looked at Karl.

He blushed. "I'm okay."

"He's more than okay. He has wonderful tone. They all do."

"And you think you can talk Vikar into performing in public?" Karl was skeptical.

"I can convince him to do anything, with the right incentive." She gave Faith a conspiratorial smile, as if another woman would understand.

To his surprise, Faith nodded.

"But that's not all. Father Bernard wants a live Nativity Scene outside the church for the week leading up to Christmas."

"Oh, crap! Well, we can't do both. Sing inside and stand outside like bleeping idiots."

"Sure we can. Those who want to sing, sing. Those who don't, can be the Three Wise Men, shepherds, Joseph, Mary, angels, whatever. I don't care if they're a jackass. And, hey, maybe baby Michael . . . that's Ivak and Gabrielle's little one," Alex explained for Faith's benefit, "could be the baby Jesus. They should be here by then."

"Alex," Karl said with a groan, "Vikar isn't going to have a bird. He's going to have a cow."

"I know," Alex said, putting her face in her hands for a moment. Then she stood. "I better go find that black negligee with the peekaboo lace."

Karl and Faith looked at each other after Alex left, then burst out laughing.

### Was she really falling in love with Dracula? . . .

Faith made it through dinner, but she didn't realize how exhausted she was until she tried to climb the first flight of stairs to her third-floor bedroom. She'd gone only five steps when Karl made a tsking sound of disgust and picked her up, as if she weighed no more than a pillow.

She liked being in Karl's arms. Too much.

"Where have you been sleeping while I've taken over your room?" she asked.

"Trond's bedroom, next door to mine, when he's in residence."

"I'm sorry to put you out. I could sleep in another room."

"It makes no difference to me where I sleep. As long as it's not a rice paddy."

"Okay," she said, and nuzzled his neck.

She thought he moaned softly, but it might have been because he was starting to feel the exertion of carrying a hundred and ten pounds up three flights of stairs. When they got to her room, he kicked the door open, turned on the lamps by nudging the wall switch with his elbow, then laid her on the bed. The light switch had also turned on the small, artificial Christmas tree Karl had bought her. It was sitting on the other side of the dresser and was possibly the most beautiful thing Faith had ever seen.

"You should take another pain pill now," Karl advised.

"Not yet," she said. "They make me sleepy, and I want to stay awake while you answer my questions."

"We could wait until tomorrow."

She shook her head. "Now."

He leaned his rump against the dresser and crossed his ankles. He wore a gray Navy SEAL T-shirt over faded denims with ratty athletic shoes.

"Are you a Navy SEAL?"

He laughed. Apparently, it wasn't the question he'd been expecting. "No. I trained to be a SEAL at one time, but that was never intended to my real mission. I *was* in the Army, but that was long before that."

His words raised more questions than answers, but there were some things she needed to get out of the way first.

"Who are you, exactly? I mean, all of you people here. Vangels?"

"How do you know about vangels?"

"The twins."

"Ah. How much did the little twerps disclose?"

"Not much." She shifted her butt up so that she was propped against her pillow, and folded her arms over her chest.

"Vangels are Viking vampire angels. Some of the five hundred or so vangels that exist in the world today were actual Vikings with swords and longships and all that stuff more than a thousand years ago. Vikar and his brothers, for example, are that old. Others, like me and Armod, aren't that old, but we have at least some Norse blood in our veins."

"Whoa! Are you saying that Vikar and his brothers are more than a thousand years old?"

"Yes."

"He doesn't look much older than his early to mid thirties."

"Vangels do not age."

"How convenient!" she said. Then narrowed her eyes at him, "How old are you?"

"Well, I was twenty-two years old when I died in Vietnam forty-two years ago. So, I guess you could say I'm sixty-four."

"Holy cow! And here I thought I was being a cougar at twenty-nine, lusting after a younger man."

He grinned. "You lust after me?"

She decided to ignore his question. For now. "That still doesn't explain the whole vangel . . . vampire angel business."

"A long, long time ago, God got angry with the Viking race as a whole, and the Sigurdsson brothers in particular. Too sinful, too vain, too vicious, too arrogant. He decided to wipe out the Viking culture and, in fact, eventually did so."

"That is some story!"

"You don't see any Viking nation today, do you?"

"I guess I never thought about it."

"At the last minute, St. Michael the Archangel interceded on their behalf, and God gave the Vikings a second chance at redemption. Some of them, anyhow. Jasper, one of the fallen angels, was wreaking havoc on earth with his Lucipires, demon vampires. God commissioned Michael to turn a band of fallen Vikings into vampire angels to fight the Lucies."

"Holy moly!"

"It's a lot more complicated than that, but I think I've given you enough information to digest, for now. You can see why secrecy is important to us, and why, at first, I tried to hide your presence here. The less you know, the less you can reveal when you leave."

Karl mentioned her leaving in such a casual manner

that it felt like a stab to the heart to Faith. She tried not to show her hurt. "Do you seriously expect me to believe you're a vampire?"

He made a hissing sound and turned to her. Fangs emerged from his mouth, and he licked his lips, like he was considering taking a good bite of her neck.

She shimmied over to the other pillow against the wall.

"See. I'm a true-blue, blood-drinking vampire." He rubbed a hand over his mouth, and his fangs receded into his gums, leaving only small, almost unnoticeable points on his incisors. "Still lust after me, baby?" There was an endearing vulnerability in his eyes as he asked the question.

"Probably," she said. "You said vampire *angel*. Do you have wings, too?"

"Not yet. Maybe never. I do have shoulder bumps, though, where they might be someday."

"This is amazing. Do you know what I thought? You'll laugh. I thought you were some kind of gang, like Hell's Angels."

"More like Heaven's Angels. Or Heaven's Other Angels."

She smiled. "I think I'll take my pills now."

He went to the bathroom, where she could hear him opening the medicine cabinet and pouring water. She hurried and undressed, pulling on her flannel nightgown. When he returned, she was in bed, under the sheets. She took the pills and drank half of the glass of water.

"I really am safe here, then?"

He nodded.

"Would you lie down with me until I fall asleep?"

"That's not a good idea."

"Why? We could bundle like the Amish do? Like we did that first night you brought me here, and you lay on top of the quilt."

"You remember that? You appeared to be unconscious."

"I remember bits and pieces." She scrooched over and patted the top of the quilt on his side. "C'mon. I promise I won't jump your bones."

"That's not what I'm worried about."

She arched her brows at him in question."

"Sweetheart, a concrete wall between us wouldn't stop me from making love to you tonight, let alone some friggin' blanket bundling."

"Maybe I should borrow Alex's negligee."

"Don't you dare!"

Faith was already falling asleep by then, but there was a smile on her face.

She thought she heard Karl mutter something about a five-mile run followed by a cold shower.

## Chapter 7

*It was a devilish time of the year, after all . . .*

JASPER HATED CHRISTMAS with a passion. That's why he was holed up in Horror, his palace in the far north. Not that ridiculous North Pole of red-coated fat guy, elves, and flying-reindeer madness. No, this was the true Arctic wilderness.

"I brought you a bloody eggnog," said Beltane, Jasper's French hordling assistant, in an attempt to cheer him up. "It's curdled just the way you like."

Jasper was lying on a chaise, staring out the icy window of his bedchamber. The chaise was specially made with a hole in its center to accommodate his tail, so that it didn't make a lumpy bulge under him. Tails were the bane of all Lucipires. That and scales that were always flaking, and red eyes that burned, and claws that could do physical damage if one forgot and scratched a body part. *Can anyone say jacking off? Ouch!* Not that Lucipires couldn't morph into humanoid form when needed. Still . . .

"Thank you, Beltane." Jasper took a sip. "Very good." He sighed with boredom and set aside the mug, his favorite, with the logo, "Sin Rocks!"

"You should be in a good mood, master," Beltane said as he began to tidy Jasper's massive bedchamber. "Your last big mission, the one in those gambling casinos, netted you almost three hundred and fifty evil humans. Most of them have already been turned into your loyal minions."

"I know." Jasper sighed again.

"Still, you are depressed." Beltane sighed, too, in sympathy.

"Yes. You have to understand, Beltane, Christmas is the worst time of the year for a demon vampire. For any demon, actually. It is a time when humans celebrate goodness and generosity and cheerfulness and all that gagsome rubbish, not to mention the birth of He whom we Lucipires prefer not to mention."

"And the music! Do not forget the constant jingle-belling," Beltane said. "And the Christmas movies that go on and on and on about giving and sharing."

Jasper rolled his eyes in agreement. "Scrooge was a hero, in my opinion, before he went all goody-goody, and the Grinch could be a role model for all children if they'd cut off the sickening, happily-ever-after ending."

"I loved that movie! Until the ending." Beltane began to sing the lyrics to the movie sound track, something about Mr. Grinch being a cruel man. At Jasper's frown, the boy stopped abruptly. "Sorry."

"That's all right." More sighing.

"Perhaps you would enjoy watching the torture of the remaining holdouts from Las Vegas. Malcolm is about to put pins in one man's eyeballs."

"Not today."

"May I make a suggestion, master?"

Actually, Jasper wished Beltane would just go away and leave him to his misery, but the boy was one of the few truly faithful followers he had left. "Certainly," he conceded.

"The humans have a saying about turning lemons into lemonade. Why not turn this distasteful time of year to your advantage?"

"How so?"

"Well, there is still evil throughout the world for us to reap, even at this time of year. Perhaps a short mission would lift your spirits."

"And you have an idea for such a mission?" Jasper asked skeptically. Beltane, bless his black heart, was not a warrior, although he would like to be one.

"I do. I do. I was reading something on the Internet."

The boy spent entirely too much time on that blasted computer.

"There is this famous cathedral in New York City—"

"St. Patrick's?"

"No. The other one. St. Ambrose's Cathedral. Five

days before Christmas, they are holding a massive penance service, at which three dozen priests will be available to hear confessions. And you know that Christmas and Easter are times when the worst sinners come out of their closets, so to speak, seeking forgiveness."

Jasper sat up with sudden interest. He was beginning to get the drift of Beltane's idea. And he liked it.

"What better opportunity for Lucipires to pick off sinners than just before they go to confession!"

Jasper clapped his clawed hands together and pierced the skin of his palms. He did not care. "I could station a few haakai and dozens of mungs at strategic places outside the cathedral. They can kill those whose sin scent is the strongest before they ever enter the holy place. Best to leave the imps and hordlings at home this time. They just create chaos. No insult to you, my boy."

"No insult taken, m'lord."

"It would have to be short and sweet, this mission," Jasper mused as he stood and began pacing. He thought best when he paced. "All done and over with in a few hours. Mayhap a dozen haakai would be better and fifty mungs. Call Zebulan. He would be good person to head this venture." Jasper paused and looked fondly at the boy. "And, Beltane, good job!"

Beltane smiled, which caused his fangs to show.

"Honestly, it's shameful that, with all my advisors, it came down to you, a mere hordling, to come up with a brilliant mission plan. Believe me, heads are going to roll at the next council meeting, and I do not mean human ones."

"Shall I call for a council meeting, too?"

"Yes. And, Beltane, I believe I *will* come watch a little torture, after all. Plus, I need to clear the killing jars to make room for all our new arrivals."

"It is good to see you happy once again."

Jasper looped an arm over Beltane's shoulder, the two of them shuffling down the corridor, tails dragging, scales flying.

"Betimes, even at Christmas, it is good to be a demon vampire," Beltane remarked.

Jasper said, 'Ho, ho, ho!"

### *Their bells jingled, but not for long . . .*

After almost a week of torture, being near Faith and wanting her so badly his fangs ached, and another body part throbbed, Karl decided it was time to get away from the castle. He asked Jogeir to ride along with him to Faith's trailer, so that he could drive Faith's VW back to the castle, assuming the bug was still there and Karl could get it to run.

Faith wanted to come with him, to get the remainder of her clothing and other belongings, but he wasn't taking a chance of her seeing Leroy again and maybe deciding to go back to him. She'd given no hint of wanting to do that, but still, Karl knew it was the pattern of abused women. Especially ones who might be pregnant and feel an obligation to the father.

They still didn't know for sure whether she was pregnant or not. Karl had purchased not one, but two pregnancy kits when he went to the mall with Alex, but he'd yet to give them to Faith. Why, he wasn't sure. But then, Faith hadn't asked for one, either. It was as if, once they knew for sure, things would change, and for now, the status quo was preferred.

One thing was for damn sure, Karl wasn't going to be jumping the bones of a pregnant woman, or even jingling her bells. Not that Faith wasn't attractive to him, but it was a line he wouldn't cross. He hoped.

"Man, it's getting cold again," Jogeir commented. "They're calling for more snow tonight."

"That's great. The last snow hasn't melted yet." In fact, huge drifts were piled on either side of the narrow road leading to the trailer park, and once Karl got to Faith's spot, he saw that her VW was covered with about twenty inches of the white stuff. There was no motorcycle in evidence, which was kind of a disappointment. Karl was in the mood for a fight.

"Home sweet home, huh?" Jogeir observed.

"You have no idea."

Karl grabbed Faith's empty suitcase, which she'd given him, and Jogeir picked up the empty boxes in the back of the trunk. The door to the trailer was unlocked.

"Holy crap!" Jogeir said on entering.

It was colder than a witch's tit in the Klondike inside, the last of the fuel probably having run out. Plus, it looked like a tornado had run through the place, or a mean-ass dude bent on pathetic revenge.

Dishes had been tossed and lay broken on the floor.

Sofa cushions ripped. The pitiful little Christmas tree ground into shreds, probably by a heavy boot. The small kitchen table was kicked over.

Pinned to the refrigerator with a Budweiser can-opener magnet was a note in a near-illegible handwriting:

Faith:
> I'm off to Nashville where I might have a record deal. I hope you die, bitch, and our baby, too. If you try to nail me for child support, I'll come back and kill you. The landlord wants his rent or you're evicted. Ha-ha. Have fun with that jarhead in the loser pickup. I'm sick of your skinny ass anyhow.
> Leroy

Karl really, really wished Leroy was still around. He crumbled the note in his hands and stuffed it in his jacket pocket. "Let's get this over with," he told Jogeir.

Fifteen minutes later, Karl was crammed into the little VW bug, following Jogeir back to the castle. Karl was going to stop at the diner and tell Jeanette that Faith was safe, but beyond that he wasn't sure what he was going to do. He wouldn't give Faith the note. No sense adding to her shame, and she *would* feel shamed by Leroy's insults, even though Leroy was the shameful one. Plus, Karl didn't want her thinking she could go back to live in that miserable trailer by herself. There was always the chance that Leroy might come back, and even if he didn't, Karl didn't like picturing her in that squalor.

When Karl told Jeanette that Faith was in a safe place,

under his protection, and that Leroy had left town to fur-
ther his music career, Jeanette scoffed. "That ain't why
the jerk left town. He came here lookin' for Faith and
threatened me when I wouldn't tell him your name and
where you live, not that I know anyway. I called 911 right
in front of his face and reported that a man named Leroy
Brown was in my diner, threatenin' to burn the place
down and me in it. The coward was out of here so fast,
he left skid marks on the linoleum floor. He put that dent
mark in the newspaper rack on the way out by kicking it.
I'm thinkin' about putting a plaque on it that says, 'Leroy
was here, and thank God he's gone!'" Jeanette grinned
with satisfaction.

When Karl got back to the castle, it was only four p.m.,
but the skies were already turning dark with the pending
storm. He was late for choir practice . . . he could hear
voices in the chapel singing "Angels We Have Heard On
High" . . . and, yes, he'd been conned into the Christmas
Eve hymn singing at St. Vladamir's Church, along with
Vikar and his brothers and a half dozen others. It was
that or be a Wise Man, freezing his ass off in an outdoor
stable the Amish man with a talent for casket making had
been commissioned to build.

Karl couldn't find Faith. What else was new? He went
to the kitchen to ask Lizzie and found the cook baking.
Again. With five empty bottles of rum lined up before her
on the counter.

*Uh-oh!* "Lizzie! What are you doing?"

"Makin' cooshies," she slurred out. "I mean, rummy

balls. Whadja think I whash makin'? Musket balls?" Then she giggled.

In the years he'd known Lizzie, Karl had never once heard her giggle. "That's a lot of booze for just cookies," he pointed out.

"Thassh silly. I put some on the fruitcakes, too. Yer s'pose to soak them buggers a li'l every night, but I figgered, what the hell! Why not do it all at once?"

He'd never heard Lizzie swear before, either. Then he noticed Esther dancing with a broom and Hester sitting on a stool with her face planted on the counter.

They were all snockered.

He smiled. "Do you have any idea where Faith is?"

"Yep," Lizzie said, and belched. "Lash I saw her, she was in the storeroom gatherin' a bucket, Spic and Span, Lysol, a mop, and a toilet brush."

"For what?" he asked, losing his patience. He was no longer amused.

"She's on the fourth floor, cleanin' bathrooms. Started down here and worked her way up. Twelve so far, lash I heard." The old lady cackled and rolled her eyes and almost toppled over before righting herself.

"Why is Faith cleaning bathrooms? We have vangel helpers for that."

"'Cause she wants to earn her keep. Says she ain't no charity case. I tol' her you would get your dander up, but—"

He didn't wait for Lizzie to finish but was up the stairs in a flash. The exasperating woman . . . Faith, not

Lizzie . . . was going to have a relapse. He found her on her
hands and knees with a brush and bucket of soapy water
in the middle of the large, old-fashioned bathroom. She
wore jeans and a pink T-shirt, pink-and-white-striped
socks, no shoes. Her hair was off her face, plaited in a
thick braid down her back, making her look like a Norse
princess . . . a Norse princess scrubbing a tile floor. Or
was that Cinderella?

"Are you crazy, woman?"

"What?'" Her head shot up with surprise.

"Why are you on the floor?"

"Because the mop doesn't get into the grout good
enough."

"That's not what I meant," he growled. "You have no
business—" He was storming toward her when his foot
slipped on the soapy surface.

Even as he was falling backward, Faith rose and tried
to catch him. A ridiculous gesture, considering the difference in sizes. She slipped, too.

He went down hard, and she landed on top of him,
equally hard.

"Damn!" he yelled, as his head hit the floor, and he
saw stars for a moment. In fact, a whole frickin' constel-
lation.

"Damn!" she yelled as she came down on him, arms
and legs flailing.

It took him only a moment to realize that she had
landed breast to chest, groin to groin, between his wide-
spread legs. And he liked it.

He smiled.

She smiled back.

He put his hands on her butt and adjusted her even better against him. Better, as in, *I wonder if my eyeballs are rolling back in my head? I wonder if her bells are jingling yet. Mine sure are.*

She braced her hands on either side of his head, which placed her small breasts right about within kissing distance of his mouth if he leaned up a little. If he were so inclined. And, boy, was he inclined!

"You're back," she said breathily.

"I'm back." *And on my back. And getting more inclined by the second. And jingling.*

"And?"

*Can we have sex? Oh, she means:* And what happened at the trailer? "I brought your stuff, what I could find, and your car. The bug is parked in the garage. Leroy is gone, and I don't think he's coming back."

She nodded.

"Do you feel bad about that?"

She shook her head. She was staring at him in the oddest way.

"What?" he asked, rubbing his open palms over her back from her shoulders to her thighs, and up again. She was starting to fill out now that Lizzie was feeding her, practically nonstop. *Lizzie! Could that be it?* "Have you been eating Lizzie's booze balls?"

"Rum balls," she corrected, "and, no, I didn't. A girl could get blitzed at fifty paces just breathing those things."

"Why do you have that little secret smile on your face?"

CHRISTMAS IN TRANSYLVANIA 93

"I found the pregnancy tests when I was dusting your room," she revealed as she nibbled at his bristly chin. He hadn't shaved that morning, not having anticipated getting his bells rung today.

"And?" He tipped her face up with a forefinger to get her full attention.

"And I'm not preggers."

*Hallelujah!* he thought, then wiped the grin off his face. "I'm sorry."

"I'm not. Do you really think I wanted to have that monster's baby? I mean, I would have had the baby and loved it, but it's better this way." She was rambling, nervously.

She had nothing on him in the nervous department. He tried to register what she was saying, but the scent of cotton candy was swirling around him. "You smell sweet enough to eat, and I've developed a sudden taste for cotton candy," he revealed.

"Maybe it's my bath gel. And you smell like peppermints again. Have you been stealing candy canes off the tree?" she teased.

"It's not candy canes, or some friggin' soap. When vangels find their life mates, they exude a scent from their pores, like an aphrodisiac. Sometimes it's honey, or ginger, or clove, or pine, but in my case, it must be peppermint. Yours is cotton candy."

"Are you saying that we're soul mates, or lifemates, or whatever you said?"

"I have no idea. I just know that I want you so bad, I ache with it." *Can anyone say jingle bells?*

"Really? How do you want me?" She cocked her head to the side.

Was she serious?

"I want you in my bed, against the wall, in the tub, under a shower, in my truck, and right now on the bathroom floor."

"That's a lot!" she said, and wiggled herself against his crotch, which was doing the happy dance. And jingling.

"The Vikings have a word for arousal. It's called enthusiasm. As in, 'My enthusiasm is rising.' or 'I'm so enthused I can scarce stand.' Baby, my enthusiasm is a rising tide. You keep jiggling like that, and you're going to be caught in the undertow."

"I can swim," she said in a small, tentative voice.

*This is so not a good idea,* he told himself.

The other side of his brain, the one with a direct line to sex central, argued, *This is the best idea we've had in a long time.*

*I'll be punished.*

*It'll be worth it.*

*Maybe we could just fool around a little, and that will be enough.*

*Enough for who, birdbrain?*

*I should be chivalrous . . . get up and walk away.*

*Chivalry, my ass!*

Faith interrupted his mental argument by quoting the refrain of a popular country music song he'd heard on the radio a short time ago, "You gonna kiss me or what?"

"Or what," he answered, and dove right in. High tide and repercussions be damned!

He kissed her like a crazy man, or a man so hungry, he couldn't get enough. Thankfully, her lip was no longer sore, or he'd be doing some damage. But, hey, she was kissing him back with equal fervor. His hands were on her rump, hers were framing his face, to hold him in place.

As if he had plans to go anywhere! He was right where he wanted to be.

Rolling over so that she was on bottom, he grabbed a few towels to put under her back so he wouldn't hurt her ribs. They were supposedly healed, but he was taking no chances. Then he spread her legs with his knees and dry-humped her a few times to get her primed.

She let out a howl of pure pleasure, letting him know she was not only primed but pumped and ready to go.

He eased his jacket off, and she had her hands under his shirt helping him shove it over his head. He reciprocated with her T-shirt and bra. For a moment, he just stared at her breasts, which were small but perfect for her thin frame. The nipples and areolas were pink. What else?

He licked his lips.

"I haven't got much," she said, as if bracing herself for some insult. "Leroy says—"

He put his fingertips to her mouth. "Don't mention his name ever again. He's gone. He never existed."

She nodded and kissed his fingertips.

"We should go to the bedroom," he suggested, even as he palmed her breasts until he felt the nipples harden.

She let out a blissful hiss, and said, "I can't wait."

"The floor's too hard for you, sweetheart."

Showing a surprising strength, she shoved him over so that he was on his back again, and she was on top, kneeling astride his thighs. He watched with a pleasure bordering on pain as she undid the button on his jeans, then slowly unzipped him. His "enthusiasm" popped up, and she laughed, an innocent, playful sound that warmed his heart.

He toed off his boots and socks, then shimmied out of his jeans and briefs, but only got as far as his knees before she grabbed his cock. Holding him in two hands, she caressed him a little, then smiled that little cat smile of hers when she noticed the bead that appeared on the tip. Clearly admiring his size, she said, "Wow!"

That one word was like the "Gentleman, start your engines" signal at a NASCAR race. He was off and running. He had her jeans and panties off so fast, she might have brushburns. He left the pink socks on because . . . *okay, sue me* . . . they were as sexy as a Victoria's Secret thong to this long-deprived farm boy.

Lifting her by the waist above his body, he smiled with pure joy, then lowered her inch by inch onto his pulsing erection. Once he could see beyond the haze of his overwhelming arousal, he realized something. "Dammit. I don't have any condoms."

He was about to lift her off him, but she shook her head. "This is a safe time."

It was probably unsafe to take chances, despite her assurances, but then he recalled that vangels were sterile. Other than not being sent to hell when he died, he finally had a reason to be thankful that he was a vangel.

"Okay. Hold on, baby. This is going to be short and sweet."

And it was. Short. Using his big hands to guide her hips into a lift-and-thrust pattern, it was three, four, five strokes, and her inner muscles were rippling around him. The stunned expression on her face was priceless, one that would be embedded in his memory forever. And it was all it took for him to arch up, lifting her with his hips, as he roared out his own climax. Sweet! Better than sweet.

For several long minutes, she lay with her face against his chest, as if listening to his thundering heartbeat. His hands were caressing her back. He could count each precious rib. He was still inside her, soft but growing again. He couldn't have that, not so soon.

He lifted her face with both hands, kissed her lips, and said, "Next time will be in bed. But first, we have a mess to clean up."

They both rose carefully and looked around them before bursting out with laughter. In the process of their frenetic mating, they must have knocked the bucket over. There was soapy water everywhere, including on themselves. Faith's braid was soppy and half-undone, her socks dripping wet. His feet squished in the water.

"Okay, in the tub with you. I'll mop up the floor with some towels."

To his surprise, she didn't argue. She was still staring at him, as if stunned. He wasn't sure if she was surprised at her own amazing orgasm or the fact that they'd done the deed at all. It couldn't be because of his prowess because no man wanted to be known for a two-minute fuck.

She was bent over the tub, naked, pouring rose-scented bath salts under the running faucets, and he was on his hands and knees, naked, mopping up soapy water, when there was a slight knock on the door, which opened. Armod popped his head in, and said, "Karl, Vikar wants you to . . . oh, boy!" He was gone in an embarrassed flash.

"Are we in trouble?" Faith asked.

"I am," he said, then added with a wicked grin, "Do I look like I care?"

After Karl joined Faith in the bubble bath, and they'd soaped themselves clean and other things in the sloshing water, they'd had to mop the floor all over again.

Faith said she was going to have a hard time explaining twelve soaking-wet towels to the laundress.

Karl told her he'd buy her a gross of new towels.

Then they went to bed and never slept. By the shimmer of the two-foot artificial tree he'd bought her with its white lights and tiny pink poinsettias, they made love and talked, and made love, took a brief rest, then did it all again. Through dinner, through the night, and before dawn, when they were both startled by a loud sound outside, overhead.

"It sounds like a million pigeons," Faith said. "Or bats."

He was spooned against her, with a sheet, a blanket, and the quilt over them to ward off the chill air.

"It's not pigeons or bats." Karl groaned. "It's archangels. Michael is here, and he must have brought some pals with him."

"Michael?" She rubbed her butt against him.

For the first time in the past thirteen hours, his enthusiasm did not rise to the occasion. He'd forgotten that Michael was coming. Now there was an erotic buzzkill!

"Michael the Archangel. Remember, I told you about him?"

She turned so that she could look at him in the dim light. "You were serious? About all that vangel/demon/vampire stuff."

"Serious as . . ." He lifted the covers to stare at their nude, much-sated bodies, ". . . sin."

"Are we in trouble?" she asked, repeating an earlier question

He gave her the same answer as before, "I am."

And, man, was that an understatement, he soon found out. Hell hath no fury like an archangel with a bone to pick, the bone being Karl.

## Chapter 8

*Angels we have heard on high, and down
below, too . . .*

EVEN THOUGH HE'D arrived at dawn, it was late morning
before Michael called for a meeting of the vangels.

Before that, Karl took a tray upstairs for Faith, with
coffee, orange juice, two buttered croissants, and a
banana. He urged her to stay put unless she was invited
to come downstairs.

"Will I be invited? I've never met an angel before.
Except for you, and you're just an almost-angel." At his
raised brows, she added, "I'm not saying this right."

"I understand perfectly," he said, and kissed her
lightly. "I'll be back as soon as I can."

Not being a VIK, Karl was able to step back and ob-
serve, for the most part. First, Michael had been engaged

in a closed-door meeting with Vikar, while Gabriel, who'd accompanied him, was in the dungeon . . . uh, basement, discussing training exercises with some of the newer vangels. Rafael led a prayer service in the chapel and listened to some of the hymns they'd been rehearsing for the Christmas Eve service. After that, they all attended Mass, celebrated by Father Bernard, who'd come up from St. Vladamir's, followed by a hearty workman's breakfast for the archangels . . . sausage, bacon, fresh-baked rolls, scrambled eggs, hash browns, and toast . . . served by Lizzie and her helpers, who were clearly suffering hangovers. Once the archangels were gone, Karl was sure the kitchen staff would be crawling into their beds. The rest of them would have to make do with Domino's Pizza or takeout the rest of the day though the storm had laid down another six inches of snow last night, and it was snowing again. Travel might be a problem, even into town for a bucket of KFC. Best they stick to home and open a can of soup or something. Not that anyone was thinking that far ahead. The vangels were too worried about why Michael was here and whether any of them was in the archangel's crosshairs.

None of the archangels were smiling, which Karl took for a bad sign. The only indication Karl had that he was in particular trouble was a frown directed his way by Michael and the one-word warning, "Later!"

The other brothers, and their families, began drifting in. Their late arrivals were excused by the fact that Michael hadn't been expected until tomorrow. Sometimes, he liked to surprise them. In an attempt to catch them doing something wrong, Karl supposed. Like Karl had been. Though it hadn't felt wrong at the time. Still didn't.

There was Trond with his wife Nicole, both Navy SEALs. Well, Trond was a SEAL, but Nicole was a member of WEALS, the female Navy SEAL unit. They were followed by Sigurd, Harek, and Mordr, whose new wife Miranda and their five children would be arriving later. And Cnut, who was being teased by his brothers because of his new hairstyle.

The light brown hair was shaved on both sides of his head. On the top, three narrow braids ran from his brow to the crown of his head, where they met in one long braid that hung down to his shoulders. He also had a neatly trimmed beard and mustache.

"Who the hell are you supposed to be?" Vikar asked.

"Travis Fimmel who plays Ragnar Lothbrok in that History Channel series called *The Vikings*," Harek answered for Cnut with a wide grin.

"You look like an idiot," Vikar observed.

"Up yours, bro," Cnut replied. "It's the latest style."

"You wouldn't know style from a pile . . . of shit," Trond contributed.

"I like it," Nicole said, and waggled her eyebrows at Cnut.

"You do?" Trond asked and rubbed his hand over his short military cut.

"You do know how Ragnar ended up in real life, don't you? King Aelle threw him in a snake pit, where he died painfully." This from Harek.

"What's your point?" Cnut asked.

"Just sayin'," Harek said, still grinning.

Then came Ivak, with his wife Gabrielle and their baby Michael. What a suck-up Ivak was, naming his child after the archangel although he claimed to have named him after Michael Jordan, the basketball player. Armod had been disappointed that the namesake hadn't been Michael Jackson. Ivak, a chaplain at Angola Prison, wore a clerical collar under a denim shirt, probably hoping to impress Michael with his piety, which was a total crock. *Did I mention suck-up?*

Finally, the meeting was convened in the front salon. Michael sat in one of the two wingback chairs facing the room, Vikar in the other. The female vangels took the remaining chairs. Everyone else was crammed into whatever space they could find, on the floor or leaning against the walls.

The archangel was in full celestial attire today . . . white robe belted with a golden rope, sandals, long, shiny, dark hair on which light reflected from the snow outside through the windows, rather like a halo. And wings. His massive white wings lay folded against his back. You never knew how Michael would show up. Sometimes he wore modern clothes, like jeans and T-shirt, and athletic shoes, which he had a passion for, with no wings at all.

"Rafael and Gabriel were called away to an emergency on Agatnor. We will proceed without them," Michael said. "Those Agats are more bothersome than Vikings. Like gnats they are betimes."

That was a sample of archangel humor, but no one laughed, just in case it was not a joke.

However, curiosity got the better of Harek, who stood next to Karl, and he dared speak, "What is Agatnor?" Harek was the brightest of all the Sigurdsson brothers, brighter than most anyone, for that matter. Not that it was very bright of him to call attention to himself by speaking unless called upon.

Karl put a hand to his face and scrunched down lower, trying to be invisible. Impossible, of course.

"Not what. Where," Michael replied, amusement tugging at his lips when he might very well have been annoyed at the interruption.

Harek tipped his head to the side. His mind was like an encyclopedia, and you could almost see the search going through it, like the computers he loved. *Agatnor? Agatnor? Agatnor?* "What continent is it on?"

Karl and others in the room braced themselves for Michael's anger. Michael was not here to play puzzle games with the Vikings, but he surprised them again. First, by being so patient with Harek. (Maybe some of the Christmas spirit was rubbing off on him.) Second, by his answer, "Agatnor is not on any continent. It is a planet."

"Are you saying that there is life on other planets?"

"Vanity, thy name is Viking," Michael said, shaking his head at their hopelessness. "Only full-of-themselves Norsemen would think the world revolved around them and only them. But on to the business at hand." Michael pulled a notebook from a pocket in his robe.

Meanwhile, Harek was muttering under his breath. "Aliens! There really are aliens. I knew it!"

After consulting his notes, Michael sniffed the

evergreen-scented air and surveyed the room. "Very nice," he concluded. "Tell Alex I am well pleased with her efforts."

Alex and her cohorts had gone overboard in decorating. Not just the tree, which was like a ginormous air freshener, but holly arrangements and trailing pine garlands and candles and mistletoe and poinsettias and dozens of gaily wrapped presents. Karl had feared that the archangel, when he finally noticed the excess, would be upset by the commercial nature of the decorating, but, at Vikar's insistence, there were also five Nativity Scenes of various sizes situated around the room. Under the tree, on the mantel, on side tables, on top of a glassed bookcase. Vikar was a suck-up, too, when need be, or maybe he was just crafty when dealing with their heavenly mentor.

Vikar nodded. "I will pass along your compliment."

"I hate to interrupt your holiday, but a mission has come up. Jasper, unfortunately, does not stop to celebrate the Lord's birth."

They all went on red alert.

"Five days before Christmas, there will be a large penance service at St. Ambrose Cathedral in New York City. Under the direction of Cardinal Santori, thirty priests are being brought in to hear confessions from the multitudes over a three-hour period." He paused so they could take in his words and ask questions, if there were any.

They had lots, but no one spoke up. Yet.

"Thou knowest that Christmas and Easter are times of the year when lapsed Christians flock to church. Ofttimes, this season of rebirth also draws the most hardened sinners. Since it is the goal of Lucipires to grab sinners before they have a chance to repent . . ." Michael let his words trail off.

"The Lucies are going to suck the poor souls dry before they have a chance to confess," Cnut guessed.

At first, Michael just gaped at Cnut's new hairstyle. Then he muttered something about, "Vikings! Fools, every one of them!"

"Ingenious, really," Sigurd commented about Jasper's plan. At Michael's frown, he added, "In a diabolical way, I mean."

"What is the source of your intel?" Trond asked. That was SEAL speak for, "Who told you?" He smiled. "Was it Zeb?"

Zebulan was a demon vampire who acted as a double agent for Michael in hopes that he could one day switch teams. He and Trond were friends, of sorts.

"It was, and since he is heading the operation for Jasper, he must be careful not to, how do they say it today? Blow his covering?" Michael really shouldn't try modern slang. He somehow always got it wrong. No one corrected him, though. Even Karl, who was closer to a modern man than most of them.

"Like the gambling-mecca missions of last summer, which gained Jasper way too many new Lucipires for my comfort." Michael comfort"—Michael glared at each of them in turn even though not all of them had been involved in that goat fuck—"this will be a small operation and short-lived. For those three hours only, Jasper will have about fifty of his best Lucipires stationed in and about the cathedral, within a one-block radius."

"They wouldn't dare go inside the church, would they?" Regina asked.

"No. Demons never cross the line into holy places."

"There are a huge number of people expected to attend this Penitential Service," Harek said. "I read about it on the Internet. They'll be coming from a lot of the surrounding parishes."

"Thou art correct, Harek. But Jasper has no interest in the majority of them. They will be scenting out the worst sinners, those guilty of grievous acts."

"I'm thinking twenty-five of us vangels should be enough," Vikar said, the light of battle brightening his face. There was nothing a Viking liked better than a good fight.

"Yes, and I am depending on you to lead this mission, with the least souls taken and the most demon vampires sent to their hellish home."

"As you say," Vikar said, bowing his head.

Just then, the sound of Alvin and the Chipmunks came blaring through the sound system.

Michael's head jerked back. "What in the name of clouds is that?"

The sound of footsteps could be heard running down the hallway toward the family room, followed by the turning off of the music, followed by a woman's voice chastising, "Who did that?" It was probably Alex scolding the twins.

Karl couldn't help but grin. The imps!

"Uh, that was probably Gunnar and Gunnora playing their favorite Christmas singing group," a red-faced Vikar disclosed.

"*That* is Christmas music?" an incredulous Michael asked. "Tsk, tsk, tsk." He stood, putting an end to the meeting. "I will want to meet with the children before I leave. You can all breathe easily. There will be no personal reckonings today."

Karl let loose with a breath he hadn't realized he'd been holding.

"Except for Karl. Mr. Mortensen, I will see you in the library in a half hour.

Karl's heart dropped. He wasn't ready to give up Faith already.

"Everyone else, have a Blessed and Happy Christmas." And he left, heading toward the sounds of children laughing.

As everyone was exiting the room, Vikar came up to him, "I assume he wants to chew your ass about Faith. Do you want me to go with you to explain why you needed to bring a human here?"

"No. It's my responsibility."

"Well, I had a hand in her staying. I could have forbidden it."

"That's not the problem," Armod, the blabbermouth, said. "It's because he and Faith were scrubbing the bathroom floor, naked."

About a dozen lingering vangels who overheard Armod's high-pitched voice stopped to stare at Karl. And as one, there was a communal, "Uh-oh!"

### *And then the Christmas visitor arrived . . .*

To her disappointment, Faith never got to meet any archangels. To her even greater disappointment, Karl had been avoiding her ever since St. Michael's visit a week ago. No explanation, just kaplooey to you, babe. *Hump me, dump me. I should be used to that by now.*

Meanwhile, the castle was abuzz with yet more holiday preparations. Christmas music playing nonstop. (But somehow, the Alvin and the Chipmunks CD had gotten lost.) More cookie baking. (There was a moratorium, though, on alcohol-laced ones.) The ordering of costumes for the live Nativity Scene. (Faith had agreed to be the Virgin Mary. Wasn't that a laugh?) Choral practice for the Christmas Eve program. (Karl really did have a nice baritone voice.) And frantic trips to town and the mall every day to buy presents. (With only twenty dollars in leftover tips, Faith had no clue what to buy for Karl, or even if she should buy him anything.)

In the midst of all this gaiety, Faith was miserable. Her body was finally healed, but her heart was breaking.

She had to make a concerted effort to hide her depression; so, she'd offered to help Alex address Christmas cards at the counter in the kitchen. Gabrielle was upstairs in her bedroom, nursing her baby, while Nicole had taken the twins to the Amish market in Belleville. The men, and some of the women vangels, were in the basement/ dungeon practicing for some kind of hush-hush vangel mission.

Vikar came up to get several bottles from the fridge. Fake-O, she'd learned, was some kind of synthetic blood. Yeech!

"What are you doing now?" Vikar demanded of his wife.

"Sending Christmas cards, from you and me and the twins."

"To whom? I can't imagine anyone who doesn't live here who'd want Christmas greetings from us." He took a long swig from one of the bottles and grimaced, before belching.

"That was rude, Scrooge," she said. "Ben Claussen, my old boss at *World Gazette* magazine in D.C. Tante Lulu in Louisiana. The Magnussons at Blue Dragon Vineyard. Our Amish friends. The mayor of Transylvania. The contractor who does all that work for you. I expect I'll send out about a hundred cards."

"For the love of a troll!" Vikar grumbled, and stomped over to Lizzie, who was stirring a huge pot on the stove. "What smells so good? Is that what I think we're having for dinner?"

"Yes! Freakin' pasta and freakin' meatballs! Again!" *Freakin'* was apparently a new word for the cook, and she used it a lot. "I don't know why you vangels keep asking for it. The spaghetti gets caught in your fangs."

"You're a vangel, too," Vikar pointed out as he dipped a hunk of bread into the sauce and took a big, appreciative bite. "Ummm, good!"

"I may be a vangel, but that don't mean I have to like freakin' pasta all the time. You'd think you were eye-tall-yans, instead of Vikings."

"You have any more of those rum balls left?"

"No. Someone hid them." She glanced pointedly toward Alex, who pretended to be studying her list.

"Oh, one more thing, Vikar," Alex said. "You haven't picked your name for the Secret Santa yet."

"The what?"

"Secret Santa. There are too many people here for us all to exchange gifts. So, everyone's name goes into a bowl, then you only have to buy one present."

"That's the dumbest thing I ever heard," Vikar as Alex shoved a fishbowl half-filled with slips of paper toward him.

He took one of the papers out, and read, "Regina."

"You fool! You're not supposed to tell anyone. It's a secret."

"I would not have a clue what to buy for Regina. I think she's brewing witchly potions up in her bedchamber again."

"Maybe you could give her some dried newts or whatever she cooks in that cauldron."

"I caught her gathering bat shit one time."

"You did not!"

He shoved his paper back in the bowl and picked another one. "That is better," he said, tucking the paper in the back pocket of his jeans. "I will buy him a new sword."

"You can't spend more than twenty dollars," she told him.

"When will we be exchanging these gifts?"

"Christmas morning. Santa will be passing them out."

He narrowed his eyes at her. "Santa?"

"Yep. Santa Claussen. A jolly old Viking soul."

"No."

"Please?"

"No."

"Honey?"

"Pfff! I'm going to need more convincing than that." On that warning note, Vikar winked and left.

"You two get along so well. How long have you been married?" Faith asked.

"Two years."

"But your children . . ." She started to say that the children were older than that.

"Gunnar and Gunnora are sort of adopted."

"Sort of?"

"It's a long story," Alex said with a laugh. "Let's just say they're Vikar's grandchildren about dozens of times removed."

That was about as clear as mud.

"And you believe all this stuff about vampire angels?"

"Hard not to when I'm sleeping with one. Happily, I might note."

"I don't understand."

"You really don't need to understand it all unless you plan on hanging around." She gave Faith a pointed look.

"Why would I do that?"

"Karl?"

"Hard to stick with a guy who won't even talk to me."

"Oh, that's just because Michael ordered him to stay away from you."

"Why would he do that?"

"The usual. Karl's a vangel. You're a human. He's sterile. You will probably want babies. If you marry, you would only live as long as he does . . . that could be a hundred days or a hundred years or hundreds of years." Alex shrugged.

"Did Michael do the same thing with you and Vikar?"

"Oh, yeah. And with Trond and Nicole, and Ivak and Gabrielle, and Mordr and Miranda."

"How did you overcome Michael's objections?"

"There's nothing like a determined Viking, that's all I can say."

"Well, that's it then. Karl isn't determined about me."

"I don't know about that. I think it's more that Karl feels he has nothing to offer you. You would be giving up too much to be with him."

"Are you kidding me? He's like gorgeous, and I'm skinny and plain as a broom. My home is a rusty old fire-trap of a trailer. I've been living with a man who beats on me. My brother was in prison, probably still is."

"I doubt Karl looks at you that way. In fact, I know he doesn't. And don't put yourself down, girl. You've had some bad luck, but you're very pretty."

Faith shrugged. "It's not fair that someone else should

decide what's good or bad for me. Seems to me that I should have some say about it."

"Well, he is an archangel."

"I meant Karl."

"That's the attitude."

Faith didn't immediately go looking for Karl. She had a lot to think about. Even if Karl did love her, even if he wanted a relationship with her, she wasn't sure she could handle this kind of life. She still had trouble believing that he was a vampire angel and all that implied.

Nicole returned to the castle with the children then, and they all somehow moved en masse to the TV lounge area, along with Gabrielle, who'd come downstairs, carrying a baby monitor, as she had left her little one napping.

Armod was there watching a *Thriller* video, which he moved to turn off, but the twins begged him to show them once again how to moonwalk. They were all soon up on their feet learning the Michael Jackson dance step. Armod had the moves down pat. The twins kept tripping over their little feet. And the rest of them were adequate at best. But Faith found herself laughing, which was a welcome change from her misery.

Then Nicole offered to teach them the latest dance popular on the West Coast. It was a combination of dirty dancing and the shag, which they did to the slow beat of "Santa Claus Is Coming to Town." Then Gabrielle taught them how to do the Cajun two-step to the very un-Cajun "Jingle Bells." By then, they were all laughing. Armod

was high-fiving those closest to him. Several others vangels had joined them, including Regina, the witch vangel.
Regina surprised them all by suggesting Pharrel Wil-
liams's happy dance. She gave Armod the evil eye when
he laughed at her.

Heck, they were all laughing, and Gunnar and Gunnora were rolling on the floor with a fit of the giggles.

"How about you, Faith?" Alex asked then. "What is
your favorite dance?"

"Well, I haven't been out dancing in ages, but I like
country music and line dancing." Soon, about twelve of
them were lined up, dipping and swaying and shimmy-
ing and wiggling their butts to the rhythm of "Jingle Bell
Rock."

At first, they didn't notice their audience, probably
because the music had been turned up so loud, but when
they clapped their hands, spun on their feet, and did a
low bump and grind, Faith heard a male voice say, "Lord
have mercy!"

It was Karl. He was standing at the forefront of a group
of men who'd come up from their mission-impossible stuff
in the basement. His jaw had dropped, and he was gaping
at her, in particular at her jeans, which were loose and had
dropped low on her hips, exposing her belly button.

*Big fat hairy deal!* "What?" she said, stopping suddenly and putting her hands on her hips. "It's a sin to
dance now?"

His mouth snapped shut. "No, but the wicked
thoughts I have watching you dance like that surely are."

"That's your problem. Not mine."

He blinked at her angry retort. Thus far, he'd only seen her meek side. She had news for him. She hadn't always been a doormat.

The others stopped, too, noticing their spectators.

"What in bloody hell are you doing now, Alex?" Vikar shouted over the booming music. "The townfolks could hear you all a mile away. Have you lost your minds?"

"Yes, and it's fun. C'mon, honey, join us."

Vikar laughed. "Not in this lifetime." He went over to turn down the music, but Trond and Ivak stopped him as they began to dance, quite expertly, with their wives.

Karl turned to Faith, and said, "I was just coming to find you when we heard the music."

"That's a likely story. You didn't have any trouble finding me the past week." She shoved past him and went out into the hall.

"Huh? Where are you going? I need to tell you something."

"I need to tell you something, too. A lot of somethings, and I'd rather not have an audience when I do. Where's my car?" She opened the door and started down the stairs leading to the dungeon-turned-basement-dormitory/TV room/exercise area. From there, she assumed there would be access to the underground parking garage.

"Why? Why do you need to find your car?"

"So I can leave."

"What? Leave? Where are you going? You can't leave. Not yet. I mean, you're going to want to stay when you hear about the surprise I have for you."

She stopped suddenly. "Another present? You avoid

me for a week, then you get me a present and think everything will be hunky-dory?"

He smiled. "Hunky-dory?"

She did not return his smile. "Could you be more clueless? A present?"

"Sort of."

"Screw your present," she said, and turned to walk away from him. They were still in the basement corridor leading toward the garages.

He grabbed her arm and yanked her into a small room that was padded with mats on the floors and walls. Some kind of combat-exercise room, she supposed. He kicked the door shut behind them.

"Faith, I have something to confess to you."

"It better be that you love me like crazy," she said, jabbing him in the chest with a forefinger.

He backed up a bit.

" . . . and you can't live without me . . ."

Another jab.

Another step back.

" . . . and it doesn't matter what Michael says. You want to marry me and make me your lifemate or soul mate or whatever the hell you call it."

She had jabbed again, this time harder, and he was backed against the wall.

"What? No! I mean, yes, that's how I feel, but it's not why I came looking for you. It's about—"

"I don't care about anything else." She rose on her tiptoes, put her hands on his shoulders, and looked up at him. "Do you love me?"

"With all my dead heart."

She growled. "If you were able, would you ask me to stay with you?"

"Of course."

"Then why aren't you determined?"

"Huh?"

"Why aren't you fighting for me?"

"Fighting whom?"

"Michael."

He groaned. "You want me to fight an archangel?"

"Not *fight* fight. Convince him that you need me."

"I do need you."

The hands that were on his shoulders wrapped around his fool neck. "I am so mad at you I could spit, but I have missed you so much. And you haven't missed me at all."

"Are you crazy? I haven't missed you?" He lifted her up so that she had to wrap her legs around his hips to keep from falling. In that position, she felt his hardness pressing against her.

Yep, he'd missed her.

He was kissing her ravenously then.

And she was kissing him back.

He turned so that she was against the padded wall. Only his erection pinned her in place because his hands were busy unbuttoning her blouse, undoing her bra, and cupping her breasts from underneath to strum the nipples with his callused thumbs. The whole time, he continued to deep-kiss her, his moans and her groans the only sounds in the room.

She reached between them and palmed his . . . *What had he called it?* . . . his "enthusiasm."

"Aaaaah!" he said, as his knees gave way. He took her with him to the padded floor. And there he showed her fifty ways to Sunday just how much he missed her.

The air swirled with the scent of peppermint and cotton candy, which should have been sickeningly sweet but was instead erotically sweet. Faith didn't think she would ever think of peppermint sticks or candy canes in the same way again. And as for cotton candy, Karl showed her with his mouth and teeth and tongue and sticky fingers just how he could eat the sweet confection . . . i.e. her.

They rolled. Him on top. Then her on top. Over and over.

He plunged.

She rode him.

He licked.

She bit.

They were on one side of the mattress floor, then the other.

In the end, she was on all fours and Karl was taking her from behind when she came to a wild crescendo of climaxes, one after another. She howled like a banshee.

Then Karl roared out his own climax.

Good thing the room was soundproof.

He collapsed on top of her, but she didn't mind his weight. Maybe she was dead, she joked with herself. She sure felt like she'd passed to the other side, of something.

"I love you," he said against her ear.

"I love you, too," she said in a muffled voice.

Laughing, he rolled over to his back, tucking her head on his chest. Her braid had come undone, and he stroked some of the loose strands off her face.

"I assume you talked with Alex, and that's what brought on this uproar," he said.

"You didn't like my uproar?"

"I loved your uproar. I'm hoping we can uproar again in a few minutes. For hours."

She smiled against his chest.

"Alex explained a lot of things about vangels and humans. The thing that bothers me is that you didn't discuss it with me. Shouldn't I have a choice?"

"In the end, Mike has the final choice, but, yes, I suppose I should have been the one to explain all the difficulties to you."

"Difficulties can be overcome. Stubborn, mulish silence can't.'

"Faith, you've been through so much. You deserve a normal life."

"What's normal in today's society?"

"Well, it sure as hell isn't eternal life glued to the side of a vampire angel who fights demons for a living."

"I kind of like being glued to you," she said, and swung a leg over his, rubbing her calf against his furred thighs.

"You're making this really hard for me," he said on a sharp inhale.

"I can tell," she said, and glanced down at his rising hardness.

"Witch!" he said, and smacked her playfully on the rump.

"Was this room a torture chamber at one time?" she asked then as she distractedly stroked the hair on his chest.

"Something like that. The dungeon is here more to be authentic to the castle idea than for any gruesome activity. The original owner was an eccentric lumber baron who built this monstrosity for his young wife, who died before she gave him any children to fill the place. I suppose he could have used this as a prison for his competitors in the lumber business, but I doubt anyone even came down here until . . . oh, my God! I forgot."

He sat up abruptly and rose to his feet. "Hurry up and get dressed."

"Why? I thought we were going—"

He was throwing he clothes at her. "I told you that I came looking for you. I told you I had a confession to make. We have a visitor."

"A Christmas visitor? Alex really is going all out with this holiday celebration, isn't she?"

"This visitor has nothing to do with Alex. Oh, man, you are going to be either so happy, or so angry."

She was dressed by now and trying to comb her fingers through her unruly hair. "Me? I'm going to be angry about this Christmas visitor?" She frowned with confusion.

"You might be angry with me for having something to do with this visitor's being here," he elaborated.

"Will you stop speaking in riddles and spit it out?"

"It's your brother."

"What?" A chill passed over her body. "Zach? That's impossible. Zach is in prison. I think."

"Not anymore. Honey, Zach is dead."

She gasped and put a hand to her heart. A tiny sob was her only vocal response.

"And he's here."

## Chapter 9

### *Off to the Big Apple . . .*

IT HAD BEEN a week since Karl had engaged in wild-
monkey sex with Faith down in the dungeon, an exercise
he had hoped to repeat a time or five, but he hardly saw
the woman. Her every spare moment was spent with her
brother Zach, a dazed, newly turned vangel.

When Karl had asked Harek to use his Internet talents to discover the whereabouts of Zachary Larson, he
had hoped to give Faith a Christmas surprise. Little did
he know it would end up being this kind of surprise. Apparently her brother had a long rap sheet, in and out of
prisons since he was a teen, most recently in Rockview
for murder. His death had come last week at the hands
of another inmate. Michael must have heard about Karl's
inquiries and turned the young man into a vangel. Zach

was the "youngest," meaning most recently turned, vangel they'd ever had though he had thirty-three hard human years under his belt.

Karl was preparing to go to New York City for the cathedral mission. The team would be gone for three days at most, staying in a whole floor of rooms rented in a small, nearby hotel for twenty-five of the vangel operators. The seven brothers, Jogeir, Svein, Armod, himself, and a dozen or so others. The initial group would study the perimeter of the church and its grounds, make specific plans and assignments. By the time Saturday afternoon rolled around, they would have a precise "battle" plan. The sulfurous scent of Lucies was supposedly already in the air.

But Karl wanted to speak with Faith before he left. He found her in the basement, where she was watching while two vangel trainers were drilling Zach on basic vangel behavior. Zach looked stunned, as well he should, especially with his new fangs cutting into his bottom lip. Other than the fangs, Zach resembled his sister in leanness and blond hair.

The trainers were teaching Zach how to retract his fangs, which was difficult at first. They repeated, over and over, the rules he must follow. Secrecy must be maintained, they emphasized. And then there was his new need for blood; his skin was almost translucent at the moment, despite their almost force-feeding him Fake-O. Soon they would show him how to feed on one of the blood ceorls here at the castle. Actual feeding in battle would be a long way off.

Karl tapped Faith on the shoulder, and whispered in her ear, "Faith, come upstairs. I need to talk with you before I leave."

"Leave?" she asked, turning to face him. The poor woman looked as if she hadn't been sleeping well. Not a good sign on top of her recent injuries.

"I have to leave on a mission. I'll be gone for a few days." He took her hand and led her upstairs, then into Vikar's office, the only room that appeared to be empty at the moment. "Promise you'll be here when I get back."

"Of course I will. Zach is here." She must have realized by the expression on his face how he felt because she added, "And you, too."

He sat down in one chair in front of the desk and motioned for her to sit in the other chair, facing him. He took her hands in his and kissed the knuckles. "I miss you."

"I miss you, too," she said, tears filling her eyes. "Oh, Karl! I'm so confused. I always dreamed . . . I always thought that someday I would find Zach and bring him home with me. That we would be a family. I knew he'd gotten in trouble. I even knew he'd been in prison, but I had no idea . . ." She let her words trail off, staring at him with hopelessness.

"Faith, this is not a bad thing. If Zach had not been turned into a vangel, he would be in a far worse place now."

"I know that. Deep down, I know that. But it's still hard to accept. I guess I don't know where I fit in all this now."

"I'm hoping it will be here. With me. And Zach."

"I don't know. I thought I did, but I don't know."

His heart sank. "Do you love me?"

She nodded.

"That's enough for now." It wasn't. Not nearly, but he would hold on to that.

"Will this mission be dangerous? I mean, is there a chance you won't come back?"

"There's always that chance."

She whimpered.

"Don't worry, honey. I have too much to live for."

"I'll be here when you get back."

### *He had a proposal to make . . .*

But Faith was not there when Karl returned two days before Christmas.

The mission had gone off with hardly a hitch. Twenty sinners saved, ten of the fifty Lucies annihilated, including two high haakai, and several vangels with serious injuries, but no vangel deaths. A success!

The twenty-five vangels returned the castle in high spirits, all looking healthily suntanned, the usual effect of feeding on sinners and trouncing Lucies. They were all looking for showers, beers, and pizza, which was supposedly on the menu tonight, and their lifemates where applicable, not necessarily in that order.

Karl now put himself in that latter category. Faith *was* his lifemate. He was convinced of that. He had an important question to ask her. But she was nowhere to be found. What was it about this confounded maze of a castle that he was always hunting for her?

When he discovered that her VW bug was missing, he became frantic with worry. What if she'd left for good? She'd threatened to find her own safe house. What if she'd departed to someplace where he could never find her.

But her brother Zach was still here. (Where else would he go?) Faith would never leave him. At least not so soon. He hoped. He found Zach watching television in the family room. He told Karl that Faith was probably shopping. She had been going out every day and returning about dinnertime.

Okay, so she had been coming back every day, but Faith didn't strike him as the shopping type, or at least not the type to spend hours at the activity. Besides, she didn't have much money, as Karl recalled. He would have to do something about that.

Alex and the other ladies were just coming in from their own shopping by the looks of them, not to mention numerous boxes of pizza. As they put the delicious-smelling pies on the counter, Karl approached. "Do you know where Faith is?"

"Working," Alex answered.

"What?"

"She's been working at the diner to earn some money for Christmas. She should be back any minute."

"Alex!" he chastised. "You let her go out on her own like that?"

"Is there a problem? I thought the nasty boyfriend was gone."

"He is, but . . ." Karl hated any reference to Leroy as Faith's boyfriend, even in the past tense. "She's not well enough to be working."

Alex laughed. "The way I hear it, she's well enough for a lot of activities."

He felt himself blush.

When Faith pulled into the back courtyard an hour later, he was outside in the blistering cold waiting for her. The minute she stepped out of her vehicle, wearing that pink jacket and ridiculous, fluffy pink hat, he said, "I should paddle your ass." And yanked her into his arms to hug her tightly.

"Is that a sexual suggestion?"

He pinched said ass, and drawled, "It could be if you want."

She laughed. "Your face and hands are freezing cold."

To punish her, he ran his cold hands under her jacket and shirt and up her bare back.

She shivered. He wasn't sure if it was because of his cold hands or his hotly talented hands. He preferred the latter.

"I've been worried about you," he growled against her neck.

"Why?"

"I thought you left."

Her eyes widened in surprise. "I told you I would be here."

"I know, but you weren't here, and I thought . . . oh, Faith, my world crashed when I thought you were gone."

"Silly man! I love you."

He smiled, weak with relief, even though she would pay later for that "silly man" remark. "I went shopping when I was in the city," he blurted out.

She had to be wondering what that had to do with his wickedly wandering hands. "Oh? I thought you hated shopping."

"Not this kind," he said, and went down on one knee. "I hadn't planned to do it like this, but damn, I'm so nervous, I can't wait. Faith Larson, will you marry me?" He pulled a small pale blue Tiffany box from his jacket pocket.

She clapped both pink-mittened hands to her heart. "Are you allowed to do that?"

"No, but I'm doing it anyway. I'll ask Mike for permission. Later. If he says no, I'll keep asking. I'm determined to have you."

She smiled. "Then yes. Yes, yes, yes."

As he slipped the diamond solitaire on her finger and stood to kiss her, they heard clapping. Turning, they saw about forty vangels, and a few humans, including two little jumping rascals, waving at them. And he could swear some of them were singing, "Another one bites the dust."

## A Very Merry Vangel Christmas . . .

Everyone agreed it was the best Christmas holiday, ever, and the first of many traditions were set that year in a Transylvania castle high on a Pennsylvania hill.

The live Nativity Scene outside St. Vladamir's Church was so successful that the townfolks who were holding their own vampire holiday events complained that so many tourists were hanging out over at the church instead of at their paying enterprises. Faith played the Virgin Mary, Ivak was Joseph, and baby Michael was the infant Jesus. Gabrielle and Nicole and Miranda were angels. Lizzie Borden held a shepherd's crook instead of an axe. The twins, Gunnar and Gunnora, were shepherds, as well. The eight-year-old twins, Ben and Sam, and five-year-old Larry, three of Mordr's adopted children, were adorable as the Three Wise Men. Mordr's other adopted children, ten-year-old Maggie and five-year-old Linda, sang in the choir. There was much laughter from the participants, as well as the spectators.

And the Christmas Eve concert at Midnight Mass was spectacular. Truly, the voices were angelic. Everyone said so.

All the children basked in numerous gifts on Christmas morning, including a new Alvin and the Chipmunks DVD some fool had given to Gunnar and Gunnora. Everyone else enjoyed their gifts, too. Karl gave Faith a car; she gave him a black negligee with peekaboo lace, which should have seemed odd, but Karl knew exactly who would be wearing the garment and who would be enjoying the gift. He didn't complain.

The best part of the holiday, some said, was the New Year's Eve wedding of Faith Larson and Karl Mortenssen. The ceremony was officiated by none other than St. Michael the Archangel in St. Vladamir's Church. The bride wore white, the groom wore his old Army dress uniform.

The wedding march was, "Angels We Have Heard On High."

Later, when someone asked Michael why he had agreed to yet another wedding amongst the vangels, he replied, "God wants all his creatures to be happy. Even Vikings."

Read on for a sneak peek at

VAMPIRE IN PARADISE

the next Deadly Angels Book
by *New York Times* best-selling author
SANDRA HILL

Available November 2014 in print
and ebook from Avon Books.

# Prologue

*The Norselands, A.D. 850 . . .*

**Only the strongest survived in that harsh
land . . .**

SIGURD SIGURDSSON SAT near the high table of King
Haakon's yule feast, sipping at the fine ale from his own
jewel-encrusted silver horn. (Many of those "above the
salt" held gold vessels, he noted.) Tuns of ale and rare
Frisian wine flowed. (His mead tasted rather weak, but
mayhap that was his imagination.)

Favored guests at the royal feast (he was mildly favored)
had their choice among spit-roasted wild boar, venison
and mushroom stew, game birds stuffed with chestnuts,

a swordfish the size of a small longboat, eels swimming in spiced cream sauce, and all the vegetable side dishes one could imagine, including the hated neeps. (Hated by Sigurd, leastways. He had a particular antipathy to turnips due to some youthling insanity to determine which lackwit could eat the most of the root vegetables without vomiting or falling over dead as a stump. He lost.) Honey oat cakes and dried fruit trifles finished off the meal for those not filled to overflowing. (Peaches, on the other hand, were fruit of the gods, in Sigurd's opinion.) Entertainment was provided by a quartet of lute players who could scarce be heard over the animated conversation and laughter. (Which was just as well; they harmonized like a herd of screech owls. Again, in Sigurd's opinion.) Good cheer abounded. (Except for . . .)

In the midst of the loud, joyous celebration, Sigurd's demeanor was quiet and sad.

But that was nothing new. Sigurd had been known as a dark, brooding Viking for many of his twenty and seven years. Darker and more brooding as the years marched on. And he wasn't even *drukkinn*.

Some said the reason for Sigurd's discontent was the conflict betwixt two warring sides of his nature. A fierce warrior in battle and, at the same time, a noted physician with innate healing skills inherited from and honed by his grandmother afore her passing to the Other World when he'd been a boyling.

Sigurd knew better. He had a secret sickness of the soul, and its name was envy. Never truly happy, never satisfied, he always wanted what he didn't have, whether it be a chest of gold; the latest, fastest longship; a prosperous estate; the finest sword. A woman. And he did whatever necessary to attain that new best thing. *Whatever.*

'Twas like a gigantic worm he'd found years past in the bowels of a dying man. Egolf the Farrier had been a giant of a burly man in his prime, but at his death when he was only thirty he'd been little more than a skeleton, with no fat and scant flesh to cover his bones. The malady had no doubt started years before innocently enough, with a tiny worm in an apple or some spoiled meat, but over the years, attached to his innards like a ravenous babe, the slimy creature devoured the food Egolf ate, and Egolf had a huge appetite, in essence starving the man to death.

"Sig, my friend!" A giant hand clapped him on the shoulder, and his close friend and *hersir* Bertim sat down on the bench beside him. Beneath his massive red beard, the Irish Viking's face was florid with drink. "You are sitting upright," Bertim accused him. "Is that still your first horn of ale that you nurse like a babe at teat?"

"What an image!" Sigurd shook his head with amusement. "I must needs stay sober. The queen may yet produce a new son for Haakon this night."

"Her timing is inconvenient, but then a yule child brings good luck." Bertim raised his bushy eyebrows as a sudden thought struck him. "Dost act as midwife now?"

"When it is the king's whelp, I do."

Bertim laughed heartily.

"In truth, Elfrida has been laboring for a day and night so far with no result. The delivery promises to be difficult."

Bertim nodded. 'Twas the way of nature. "What has the king promised you for your assistance?"

"Naught much," Sigurd replied with a shrug. "Friendship. Lot of good that friendship does me, though. Dost notice I am not sitting at the high table?"

"And yet that arse licker Svein One-Ear sits near the king," Bertim commiserated.

*I should be up there. Ah, well. Mayhap if I do the king this one new favor . . .* He shrugged. The seating was a small slight, actually.

A serving maid interrupted them, leaning over the table to replenish their beverages. The way her breasts brushed against each of their shoulders gave clear signal that she would be a willing bed partner to either or both of them. Bertim was too far gone in the drink and too fearful of the wrath of his new Norse wife, and Sigurd lacked interest in services offered so easily. The maid shrugged and made her way to the next hopefully willing male.

Picking up on their conversation, Bertim said, "The friendship of a king is naught to minimize. It can be priceless."

Sigurd had reason to recall Bertim's ale-wise words later that night, rather in the wee hours of the morning, when Queen Elfrida, despite Sigurd's best efforts, delivered a deformed, puny babe, a girl, and Sigurd was asked by the king, in the name of friendship, to take the infant away and cut off its whispery breath.

It was not an unusual request. In this harsh land, only the strongest survived, and the practice of infanticide was ofttimes an act of kindness. Or so the beleaguered parents believed.

But Sigurd did not fulfill the king's wishes. Leastways, not right away. Visions of another night and another life-or-death decision plagued Sigurd as he carried the swaddled babe in his arms, its cries little more than the mewls of a weakling kitten.

Despite his full-length, hooded fur cloak, the wind and cold air combined to chill him to the bone. He tucked the babe closer to his chest and imagined he felt her heart beat steady and true. Approaching the cliff that hung over the angry sea, where he would drop the child after pinching its tiny nose, Sigurd kept murmuring, " 'Tis for the best, 'tis for the best." His eyes misted over, but that was probably due to the snowflakes that began to flutter heavily in front of him.

He would do as the king asked. Of course he would. But betimes it was not such a gift having royal friends.

Just then, he heard a loud voice bellow, "*Sigurd!* Halt! At once!"

He turned to see the strangest thing. Despite the blistering cold, a dark-haired man wearing naught but a long, white, rope-belted gown in the Arab style approached with hands extended.

Without words, Sigurd knew that the man wanted the child. To his surprise, Sigurd handed over the bundle that carried his body heat to the stranger.

"Take her, Caleb," the man said to yet another man in a white robe who appeared at his side.

"Yes, Michael." Caleb bowed as if the first man were a king or some important personage.

*More kings! That is all I need!*

The Michael person passed the no-longer-crying infant to Caleb, who enfolded the babe in what appeared to be wings, but was probably a white fur cloak, and walked off, disappearing into the now heavy snowfall.

"Will you kill the child?" Sigurd asked, realizing for the first time that he might not have been able to do it himself. Not this time.

"Viking, will you never learn?" Michael asked.

He said "Viking" as if it were a bad word. Sigurd was too stunned by this tableau to be affronted.

"Who are you? *What* are you?" Sigurd asked as he noticed the massive white wings spreading out behind the man.

"Michael. An archangel."

Sigurd had heard of angels before and seen images on wall paintings in a Byzantium church. "Did you say arse angel?"

"You know I did not. Thou art a fool."

No sense of humor at all. Sigurd assumed that an *arch*angel was a special angel. "Am I dead?"

"Not yet."

That did not sound promising. "But soon?"

"Sooner than thou could imagine," he said without the least bit of sympathy.

*Can I fight him?* Somehow, Sigurd did not think that was possible.

"You are a grave sinner, Sigurd."

*He knows my name.* "That I freely admit."

"And yet you do not repent. And yet you would have taken another life tonight."

"Another?" Sigurd inquired, although he knew for a certainty what Michael referred to, and it was not some enemy he had covered with sword dew in righteous battle. But how could the man—rather angel—possibly know what had been Sigurd's closely held secret all these years? No one else knew.

"There are no secrets, Viking," Michael informed him.

*Holy Thor! Now he is reading my mind!*

Before Sigurd could reply, the snow betwixt them swirled, then cleared to reveal a picture of himself as a boyling of ten years or so bent over his little ailing brother Aslak, a five-year-old of immense beauty, even for a male child. Pale white hair, perfect features, a bubbling, happy personality. Everyone loved Aslak, and Aslak loved everyone in return.

Sigurd had hated his little brother, despite the fact that Aslak followed him about like an adoring puppy. Aslak was everything that Sigurd was not. Sigurd's dull brown hair only turned blond when he got older and the tresses had been sun-bleached on sea voyages. His facial features had been marred by the pimples of a youthling. He had an unpleasant, betimes surly, disposition. In other words, unlikable, or so Sigurd had thought.

Being the youngest of the Sigurdsson boys, before Aslak, and the only one still home, Sigurd had been more aware of his little brother's overwhelming popularity. In truth, in later years, when others referred to the seven

Sigurdsson brothers, they failed to recall that at one time there had been eight.

Sigurd blinked and peered again into the swirling snow picture of that fateful night. His little brother's wheezing lungs laboring for life through the long pre-dawn hours. His mother, Lady Elsa, had begged Sigurd to help because, even at ten years of age, he had healing hands. Sigurd had pretended to help, but in truth he had not employed the steam tenting or special herb teas that might have cured his dying brother. Aslak had died, of course, and Sigurd knew it was his fault.

Looking up to see Michael staring at him, Sigurd said, "I was jealous."

Michael shook his head. "Nay, jealousy is a less than admirable trait. Your sin was the more grievous, envy."

"Envy. Jealousy. Same thing."

"Lackwit!" Michael declared, his wings bristling wide like those of a riled goose. "Jealousy is a foolish emotion, but envy destroys the peace of the soul. When was the last time you were at peace, Viking?"

Sigurd thought for a long moment. "Never, that I recall."

"Envy stirs hatred in a person, causing one to wish evil on another. That was certainly the case with your brother Aslak. And with so many others you have ma-ligned or injured over the years."

Sigurd hung his head. 'Twas true.

"Envy causes a person to engage in immoderate quests for wealth or power or relationships that betimes defy loyalty and justice."

Sigurd nodded. The archangel was painting a clear picture of him and his sorry life.

"The worst thing is that you were given a treasured talent. The gift of healing. Much like the saint physician Luke. But you have disdained it. Abused it. And failed to nourish it for a greater good."

"A saint?" Sigurd was not a Christian, but he was familiar with tales from their Bible. "You would have me be as pure as a saint? I am a Viking."

"Idiots! I am forced to work with idiots." Michael rolled his eyes. "Nay, no one expects purity from such as you. Enough! For your grave sins, and those of your six brothers . . . in fact, all the Vikings as a whole . . . the Lord is sorely disappointed. You must be punished. In the future, centuries from now, there will be no Viking nation, as such. Thus sayeth the Lord," Michael pronounced. "And as for you Sigurdsson miscreants . . . your time on earth is measured."

"By death?"

Michael nodded. "Thou art already dead inside, Sigurd. Now your body will be, as well."

So be it. It was a fate all men must face, though he had not expected it to come so soon. "You mention my brothers. They will die, too?"

"They will. If they have not already passed."

Seven brothers dying in the same year? This was the fodder of sagas. Skalds would be speaking of them forevermore. "Will I be going to Valhalla, or the Christian Heaven, or that other place?" He shivered inwardly at the thought of that last fiery fate.

"None of those. You are being given a second chance."

"To live?" This was good news.

Michael shook his head. "To die and come back to serve your Heavenly Father in a new role."

"As an angel?" Sigurd asked with incredulity.

"Hardly," Michael scoffed. "Well, actually, you would be a vangel. A Viking vampire angel put back on earth to fight Satan's demon vampires, Lucipires. For seven hundred years, your penance would be to redeem your sins by serving in God's army under my mentorship."

Sigurd could tell that Michael wasn't very happy with that mentorship role, but he could not dwell on that. It was the amazing ideas the archangel was putting forth.

"Do you agree?" Michael asked.

Huh? What choice did he have? The fires of Hell, or centuries of living as some kind of soldier. "I agree, but what exactly is a vampire?"

He soon found out. With a raised hand, Michael pointed a finger at Sigurd and unimaginable pain wracked his body, including his mouth where the jaw-bones seemed to crack and realign themselves, emerging with fangs, like a wolf. He fell to his knees as his shoulder blades also seem to explode as if struck with a broadsword.

"Fangs? Was that necessary?" he gasped, glancing upward at the celestial being whose arms were folded across his chest, staring down at him.

"You'll need them for sucking blood."

"From what?"

"What do you think? From a peach? Idiot! From people . . . or demons."

"*What?* Eeew!" *He expects me to drink blood? From living persons? Or demons? I do not know about this bargain.*

"Thou can still change thy mind, Viking," Michael said.

*Reading my mind again! Damn!* "And go to Hell?"

"Thou sayest it."

Sigurd thought about negotiating with the angel, but knew instinctively that it would do no good. He nodded. "It will be as you say."

Moments later, when the pain subsided somewhat, the angel raised him up and studied him with icy contempt, or was it pity? "Go! And do better this time, vangel."

On those words, Sigurd fell backward and over the cliff. Falling, falling, falling toward the black, roiling sea. He discovered in that instant that there was one thing a vangel didn't have. Wings.

# Chapter 1

*Florida, 2015*

***Sometimes life throws you a lifeline, sometimes a lead sinker . . .***

No one watching Marisa Lopez emerge from the medical center in downtown Miami would have guessed that she'd just been delivered a death blow. Not for herself, but for her five-year-old daughter, Isobel.

Marisa had become a master at hiding her emotions. When she'd found out she was pregnant midway through her junior year at Florida State and her scumbag boyfriend Chip Dougherty skipped campus faster than his two-hundred-dollar running shoes could carry him. When her hopes for a career in physical therapy went down the tubes. When she'd found out two years ago that her sweet baby girl had an inoperable brain tumor. When the blasted tumor kept growing, and Izzie got sicker and sicker. When Marisa had lost her third job in a row because of missing so many days for Izzie's appointments. And now . . . well, she refused to break down now, either, not where others could see.

And there *were* people watching. Looking like a young Sophia Loren, not to mention being five-eleven in her three-inch heels, she often got double takes, and the occasional wolf whistle. And she knew how to work it, especially when tips were involved at the Palms Health Spa, where she was now employed as a certified massage therapist, as well as the salsa bar where she worked nights at a second job. Was she burning the candle at both ends? Hell, yes. She wished she could do more.

Slinging her knockoff Coach bag over one shoulder, she donned a pair of oversize, fake Dior sunglasses. Her scoop-necked, white silk blouse was tucked into a black pencil skirt, belted at her small waist with a counterfeit red Gucci belt. Walking briskly on pleather Jimmy Choo knockoffs, she made her way down the street to her car parked on a side street—a ten-year-old Ford Focus. Not quite the vehicle to go with her seemingly expensive attire, a carefully manufactured image. Little did folks know that hidden in her parents' garage was a fortune in counterfeit items, from Rolex watches to Victoria's Secret lingerie, thanks to her jailbird brother, Steve. A fortune that could not be tapped because someone besides her brother would end up in jail. *Probably me, considering the bad-luck cloud that seems to be hanging over my head.*

It wasn't against the law to wear the stuff, just so long as she didn't sell it. To her shame, she'd been tempted on more than one occasion this past year to do just that. Desperation trumps morality on occasion. So far, she hadn't succumbed, though all her friends knew where to come when they needed something "special."

Her parents had no idea what was in the green-lidded bins that had been taped shut with duct tape. They probably thought it was Steve's clothes and other worldly goods. Hah!

Once inside her car, with the air conditioner on full blast, Marisa put her forehead on the steering wheel and wept. Soul-searing sobs and gasps for breath as she cried out her misery. Marisa knew that she had to get it all out before she went home, where she would have to pretend optimism before Izzie, who was way too perceptive for her age. Marisa's parents, on the other hand, would need to know the prognosis. They would be crushed, as she was.

A short time later, by midafternoon, with her emotions under control and her makeup retouched, Marisa walked up the sidewalk to her parents' house. She noticed that the Lopez Plumbing van wasn't in the driveway, so her father must still be at work. Good. Marisa didn't need the double whammy of both parents' reaction to the latest news. One at a time would be easier.

Marisa had moved into her parents' house, actually the apartment over the infamous garage, after Izzie's initial diagnosis two years ago—to save money and take advantage of her parents' generous offer to babysit while Marisa worked. Her older brother, Steve, who had been the apartment's prior occupant, was already in jail by that time, serving a two-to-six for armed robbery. The idiot had carried an old Boy Scout knife in his pocket when he'd stolen the cash register receipts at the 7-Eleven. Ironically, he'd never been nabbed for selling counterfeit goods—his side job, so to speak.

Unfortunately, this wasn't Steve's first stint in the slammer, although it was his first felony. She hoped he learned something this time, but she was doubtful.

Marisa used her key to enter the thankfully air-conditioned house. Immediately, her mood lightened somewhat in the home's cozy atmosphere. Overstuffed sofa and chair. Her dad's worn leather recliner that bore the imprint of his behind from long years of use. And the smell . . . ah! The air was permeated with the scent of olive oil, onions, and green peppers, along with dark, rich Cuban coffee. It was Monday, so it must be *ropa vieja*, or shredded beef, her father's favorite, which would be served over rice with freshly toasted Cuban bread with warm butter. Knowing her mother, there would be *natilla* for dessert.

Izzie was asleep on the couch where she'd been watching cartoons on the television that had been turned to a low volume. *Mima* was a stickler for the afternoon siesta. The pretty, soft, pink and lavender afghan her grandmother had crocheted covered her from shoulders to bare feet, but her thin frame was still apparent. There were dark smudges beneath her eyes. Even so, she was cute as a button with her ski-jump nose and rosebud mouth, thanks to her father. But then, she'd inherited a Latin complexion, dark dancing eyes, and a frame that promised to be tall from Marisa, who was no slouch in the good looks department, if she did say so herself. No doubt about it, Izzie was destined to be a beauty when she grew up. If she ever did.

Marisa put her bag on the coffee table and leaned down to kiss the black curls that capped her little girl's head. She and her daughter shared the same coal-black hair, but Marisa's was thick and straight as a pin. At one time, Izzie had sported a wild mass of dark corkscrew curls, all of which had been lost in her first bout of radiation. A wasted effort, the radiation had turned out. To everyone's surprise, especially Izzie's, the shorter hairdo suited her better.

With a deep sigh, Marisa entered the kitchen.

Her mother was standing at the counter, shredding with a fork the flank steak she'd slow cooked in special seasonings all day. She wore her standard daytime "uniform": a richly embroidered apron covered a blouse tucked into stretchy waist slacks, and curlers on her head. Soon she would shower with her favorite soap from Spain, "Maja," and change to a dress, control-top panty hose, and medium pumps, her black hair all fluffed out, lipstick and a little makeup applied, to greet Daddy when he got home. It was a ritual she had followed every single day since her marriage thirty-two years ago. Just as she maintained her trim, attractive figure at fifty-nine. To please Daddy, as much as herself.

As for her father . . . even with the little paunch he'd put on a few years back and a receding hairline, when he walked into the house wearing his plumbing coveralls, Marisa's mother had been known to sigh and murmur, "Men in uniform!"

Marisa's mother must have sensed her presence because she turned abruptly. At first glance, she gasped and put a hand to her heart. No hiding anything from a mother.

"Oh, Marisa, honey!" her mother said. Making the sign of the cross, she sat down at the kitchen table and motioned for Marisa to sit, too.

First-generation Cuban Americans, they'd named their firstborn child Estefan Lopez. He became known as Steve. Marisa Angelica, who came five years later—a "miracle baby" for the couple who'd been told there would be no more children—was named after Abuela Lopez "back home," and Tia Angelica, who was a nun serving some special order in the Philippines.

"Tell me," her mother insisted.

"Dr. Stern says the tumor has grown, only slightly, in the past two months, but her brain and other tissue are increasing like any normal growing child and pressing against . . ." Tears welled in her eyes, despite her best efforts. "Oy, Mima! He says, without that experimental surgery, she only has a year to live. And even with the surgery, it might not work."

Izzie's only hope, and it was a slim one at best, was

some new procedure being tried in Switzerland. Because it was experimental and in a foreign country, insurance would not cover the expense. Marisa had managed to raise an amazing hundred thousand dollars through various charitable endeavors, but she still needed another seventy thousand dollars. That seventy thou might just as well be a hundred million, considering Marisa's empty bank account, as well as that of her parents, who'd second-mortgaged their house when Steve got into so much trouble.

She and her mother both bawled then. What else could they do? Well, her mother had ideas, of course.

After drying Marisa's tears with a handkerchief she always kept in her bra, her mother poured them both cups of café con leches, her special brewed coffee with steamed milk. No fancy-pancy (her mother's words) Keurig or other modern devices for the old-fashioned lady. They both put one packet of diet sugar and a dollop of milk in their cups before taking the first sip. A small plate of galletas completed the picture.

"First off, we will pray," her mother declared. "And we will ask Angelica to pray for Izzie, too."

"Mima! With the hurricane that hit the Philippines last year, Tia Angelica has way too much on her prayer schedule."

"Tsk, tsk!" her mother said. "A nun always has time for more prayers. And I will ask my rosary and altar society ladies to start a novena. A miracle, that is what we need."

Marisa rolled her eyes before she could catch herself.

Her mother wagged a forefinger at her. "Nothing is impossible with prayer."

It couldn't hurt, Marisa supposed, although she was beginning to lose faith, despite being raised in a strict Catholic household. Hah! Look how much good that moral upbringing had done Steve.

That wasn't fair, she immediately chastised herself. Steve brought on his problems, and was not the issue today. Izzie was. Besides, who was she to talk. Having a baby without marriage. "Okay, Mima, we'll pray," she conceded. *If I still can.*

She let the peaceful ambience of the kitchen fill her then. To Cubans, the kitchen was the heart of the home, and this little portion of the fifty-year-old ranch-style house was indeed that. The oak kitchen cabinets were original to the house, but the way her mother cleaned, they gleamed with a golden patina, like new. Curtains with embroidered roses framed the double window over the sink. In the middle of the room was an old aluminum table that could seat six, in the center of which was a single red rose in a slim crystal vase, the sentimental weekly gift from her father to her mother. The red leather on the chair seats had been reupholstered twice now by her father's hands in his tool room off the garage. A Tiffany-style fruited lamp hung over the table.

A shuffling sound alerted them to Izzie coming toward the kitchen. Trailing the afghan in one hand and her favorite stuffed animal, a ratty, floppy-eared rabbit named Lucky, in the other, she didn't notice at first that her mother was home.

Marisa stood. "Well, if it isn't Sleeping Beauty!"

"Mima!" Dropping the afghan and Lucky, she raced into Marisa's open arms. Marisa twirled Izzie around in her arms until they were both dizzy. She dropped down to the chair again, with Izzie on her lap, both of them laughing. "Dizzy Izzie!" her daughter squealed, like she always did.

"For you, Isabella." Her mother placed before Izzie a plastic Barbie plate of chocolate-sprinkled sugar cookies and a matching teacup of chocolate milk. Her mother would have already crushed some of the hated pills into the milk.

"I'm not hungry, Buelita," Izzie whined, burying her face against Marisa's chest.

"You have to eat something, honey. At least drink the milk," Marisa coaxed.

After a good half hour of bribing, teasing, singing, and game playing, she and her mother got Izzie to eat two of the cookies and drink all of the milk.

"What did the doctor say?" Izzie asked suddenly.

*Uh-oh!* Izzie knew that Marisa had gone to the medical center to discuss her latest test results. "Dr. Stern said you are growing like a weed. No, he said you are growing faster than Jack and the Beanstalk's magic beans." At least that was true. She was growing, despite her loss of weight.

Izzie giggled. "I'm a big girl now."

"Yes, you are, sweetie," Marisa said, hugging her little girl warmly.

*Somehow, someway, I am going to get the money for Izzie,* Marisa vowed silently. *It might take one of my mother's miracles, but I am not going to let my precious little girl die. But how? That is the question.*

The answer came to her that evening when she was at La Cucaracha, the salsa bar where she worked a second job as a waitress and occasional bartender. Well, a possible answer.

"A porno convention?" she exclaimed, at first disbelieving that her best friend, Inga Johanssen, would make such a suggestion.

"More than that. The first ever International Conference on Freedom of Expression," Inga told her.

"Bull!" Marisa opined.

They were in a back room of the restaurant, talking a break. They wore the one-shouldered, knee-length black salsa dresses with ragged hems, La Cucaracha's uniform for women (the men wore slim black pants and white shirts). They were both roughly five foot eight, but otherwise completely different. Where Marisa was dark and olive-skinned, Inga was blond and Nordic. Where Marisa's figure was what might be called voluptuous, Inga's was slim and boy-like, except for the boobs she bought last year. The garments they wore were not meant to be revealing but to accommodate the restaurant's grueling heat due to the energetic dancing. They needed a break occasionally just to cool off.

Inga waved a newspaper article at her and read aloud, *"All the movers and shakers in the freedom of expression industry will be there. Multibillion-dollar investors, movie producers, Internet gurus, actors and actresses, store owners, franchisees—"*

"Franchisees of what?" Marisa interrupted. "Smut?"

Inga made a tsking sound and continued, *"—sex toy manufacturers, instructors on DIY home videos—"*

"What's DIY?" Marisa interrupted again.

"Do it yourself."

"Oh good Lord!"

*"Martin Vanderfelt—"*

"A made-up name if I ever heard one."

"Please, Marisa, give me a chance."

Marisa made a motion of zipping her lips.

*"Martin Vanderfelt, the conference organizer, told the* Daily Buzz *reporter, 'Our aim is to remove the sleaze factor from pornography and gain recognition as a legitimate professional enterprise serving the public. Freedom of Expression. FOE.'"*

Marisa rolled her eyes but said nothing.

"This is the best part. It's being held for one week on a tropical island off the Florida Keys. Grand Keys, a plush special events convention center, offers all the amenities of a four-star hotel, including indoor and outdoor pools, snorkeling and boating services, beauty salons and health spas, numerous restaurants with world-class cuisines, nightclubs, tennis courts—"

"I'd like to see some of those overendowed porno queens bouncing around on a tennis court," Marisa had to interject.

Inga smiled.

"I thought they always held the pornography thing every year in Las Vegas."

"The expo is held there, but that's more for public show. They have booths and stuff and even an awards show like the Oscars. This is more for industry insiders."

"Inside, all right," she said with lame humor.

"So cynical! Becky Bliss will be there. You know who she is, don't you?"

Even Marisa knew Becky Bliss. She was the porno princess famous for being able to twerk while on top, having sex. "Are you suggesting we might learn how to do *that*?"

"It wouldn't hurt. Maybe it would enhance your non-existent sex life."

"Not like *that*!"

"Okay. Besides, Lance Rocket will be there, too."

Marisa had no idea who Lance Rocket was, but she could guess.

"Anyhow, this conference isn't for your everyday Joe, the porn aficionado. It costs five thousand dollars to attend. The only access to the island is by water. They expect to see lots of yachts and seaplanes."

Marisa was vaguely aware of the private islands comprising the Florida Keys: an unbelievable seventeen hundred islands, some inhabited, others little more than mangrove and limestone masses. The islands lie along the Florida Straits dividing the Atlantic Ocean from the Gulf of Mexico.

"Okay, I give up. Why would you or I even consider something like this? Oh my God! You're not suggesting I make porno films to raise money for Izzie, are you?"

"Of course not. Look. This article says they're looking to hire employees for up to two weeks at above-scale wages, all expenses paid, including transportation. Everything from waiters and waitresses to beauticians to diving instructors . . . even a doctor and nurse. Waiters and waitresses can expect to earn at least ten thousand dollars, and that doesn't include tips, which could add another twenty K or more. Upper-scale professions, much more."

"Why would a hotel have to hire so many employees for just one event? Wouldn't they have a staff in place?"

"The company that owns the island went bankrupt last year, and the property is in foreclosure. In the meantime, until it is sold, the bank rents it out at an exorbitant amount. You know how abandoned properties deteriorate or get vandalized. Plus, the bank probably hopes one of the wealthy dudes or dudettes who attend this thing might fall in love with the place."

"You know an awful lot about Grand Keys Island."

Inga shrugged. "I checked it out on the Internet. Hey, here's an idea. You could even work as a massage therapist. Betcha lots of these porno stars need to work out the kinks. The *big* ones would leave hundred-dollar tips." She grinned impishly at Marisa.

Marisa couldn't be offended at Inga's teasing her about the popular misconception of professional masseurs and masseuses. "Kinks . . . that about says it all. Pfff! Can you imagine what they would expect of a massage therapist at one of these events?" She lowered her voice to a deep baritone and added, " 'My shoulders are really tight, honey, and while you're at it, check out down yonder.' "

Inga laughed. "I'm just saying. If you worked as many hours there, let's say double shifting between waitressing and therapy, you might very well earn close to thirty thousand dollars. In less than two weeks! When opportunity comes down the street, honey, jump on the bus."

"You say opportunity, I say bad idea. Honestly, Inga, I can't see us doing something like this."

"Why not? We don't have to like all the people that come to the salsa bar, but we still serve them food and drinks."

"I don't know," Marisa said.

"There's something else to consider."

"If you're going to suggest that I might find a sugar daddy to pay for Izzie's operation, forget about it." *But don't think that idea hasn't occurred to me.*

"No, but there will be lots of Internet types there. Maybe you could find someone with the technical ability to set up a website for Izzie to raise funds."

"I already tried that, but every company I contacted said it has been overdone. There's no profit for them."

"Maybe you've made the wrong contacts. Maybe if you met someone one-on-one . . . I don't know, Marisa, isn't it worth a try?" Inga was serious now.

"I'll think about it," Marisa said, to her own surprise.

"Applications and interviews for employment are being held at the Purple Palm Hotel in Key West next Friday," Inga pointed out. "Don't think too long."

"Don't push."

They heard the salsa band break out in a lively instrumental with a rich Latin American beat. A prelude to the beginning of another set of dance music.

As they headed back to work, Inga said, "I'll drive."

New to Sandra's Vangels?
Find out where it all began!
Read on for a look at

## KISS OF PRIDE

the first Deadly Angels novel!

Available now in print and
ebook from Avon Books.

# Prologue

## Long ago in the icy North . . .

OUT OF THE barren glaciers and snowcapped mountains, fjords emerged like shimmering snakes, and a god-like race was created.

Tall men with glorious features. Strength to survive the harsh climate. Wicked smiles to lure women to their frigid lairs. Superb lovemaking talents perfected over long winter nights. Brave fighting skills to defend their homeland.

These seafaring warriors came to be called Vikings.

And God was pleased. Some said these Men of the North were like angels on earth (which really annoyed some angels Up There).

For three hundred years they reigned, until God realized how arrogant and bloodthirsty they had become, not to mention their worshipping false gods, like Odin and Thor. Then, one Viking family displeased Him mightily. The Sigurdssons. Not only did Sigurd the Vicious participate in the infamous raid on Lindisfarne, a Saxon monastery, but his seven sons offended God by each committing one of the seven deadly sins in a most heinous manner.

Lust. Gluttony. Greed. Sloth. Wrath. Envy. Pride.

"I am deeply disappointed in the Vikings. I made them proud examples of a favored race." Lightning bolts shot from God's hands, which He raised on high, and the clouds wept.

"Michael!" God called out, and immediately appeared the Archangel Michael, feathers flying as he rushed to His side.

Without words, Michael could see down below to what had so offended his Lord. "Tsk, tsk!" was the best he could come up with.

"Let it be known henceforth that the Viking race, male and female, will fade into extinction. Furthermore, for their wickedness, these seven sinners are condemned to Hell for all eternity. Take care of it for me."

St. Michael, who was the patron of warriors everywhere, decided to intercede on their behalf, despite his having no liking for the full-of-themselves Norsemen. "I agree that these Sigurdsson men have gone too far, but maybe they would change if given a second chance. On the other hand . . ." Already he was wishing he had bitten his angelic tongue.

Still, he reminded God that Sigurd was the seventh son of a seventh son and that Sigurd in turn begat seven sons of his own. Ivak, Trond, Vikar, Harek, Sigurd, Cnut, and Mordr. Seven was a number of import in holy circles, sacred and magical.

"I am touched by your plea, Michael, but this family has to be punished. After all, I banished Adam from the Garden of Eden for a much lesser sin."

Michael bowed his head, waiting for his orders.

After much thought, God proclaimed, "This I say unto you, the Viking race will dwindle off into nonexistence, but not by death. No, they will blend into other cultures, losing their identity. Their pride is too great to stand alone. Hereafter, no one will worship Norse gods ever again."

"As you say, Lord." Michael paused before asking, "And the seven Sigurdsson sons?"

"These seven sinners must prove themselves sevenfold. By sins they were judged, by grace they will be saved. For seven hundred years, they must roam the earth doing good works. If they fail, Satan may have them for his unholy domain."

"Shall they be priests, or missionaries?"

"No, that would be too obvious. And too easy."

And then Michael knew.

Satan had recently delegated his comrade-in-rebellion Jasper to unleash on the earth creatures of the most evil nature. Lucipires . . . Lucifer's vampires. These vultures fed on human souls, no longer allowing free will to play itself out. Instead, they swooped in before a sinner had a chance to repent, thus ensuring a hellish eternity. Why couldn't good vampires be created to save those prey to the dark legions before they did their unholy work?

God loved Michael's idea. "You will head this enterprise. Viking vampire angels. Well, not really angels. More like angels-in-training."

The archangel gasped with horror at his mistake. "Oh, not me, Lord. I have to help St. Peter repair the Pearly Gates. And Noah is building another ark. We have no room to put another ark. And those hippos! Phew!"

God frowned.

Michael sank to his knees and nodded his head in assent.

God's frown was a frightful thing, like a lash to the soul. Besides, Michael was the one who had cast Lucifer, the fallen angel now known as Satan, from Heaven. But then God's expression softened. After all, Michael was one of His favorites. "Who better than you to lead these angelic vampire soldiers?" God asked softly.

*Angelic? Vampires being angelic? Hah! And Vikings? Really, Vikings being angelic? Hah!*

Michael rolled his eyes and wished he had kept his mouth shut.

### Thy will be done . . .

Thus was born in the year 850 a band of Viking vampires, a mere two hundred or so years from the time when the Northmen would begin to disappear from the earth.

These vampires, known as the VIK, were different from any other vampires because they were made by God.

Some said they were fallen angels . . . the darkest of all God's angels.

Others said they were God's sign of hope for all mankind. Redemption.

The Sigurdsson brothers, who were thereafter referred to as The Seven, or the VIK, thought they were God's joke on the world.

They were all right.

### And then he saw the light . . .

Vikar awoke, as if from a deep sleep. The air was still around him, and he was alone on a vast plain with not a tree or fjord in sight. The skies were dark as pitch.

It felt as if every bone in his body was shattered when he slowly sat up. Glancing downward, he realized that he was naked.

Not even his trusted sword Death Flame was at hand.

With what must be hysterical irrelevance, he noted that Death Flame was a highly prized damascened sword made by the pattern-welded process with two different colored metals twisted and refired over and over until the final blade had a design on it. In his case, flames.

What *was* relevant was that the sword was worth a fortune. He never went anywhere without it.

But wait. There was a light approaching. A light so

bright he was blinded for a moment. Then the blaze of light faded to a shimmering glow, especially about the head of the most glorious-looking creature. A man, about his height, but beauteous of features. He wore a long, white, belted robe, but even so Vikar could see he was built like a warrior . . . a warrior with the face of an angel.

That should have been a clue, but betimes Vikar was thickheaded.

"Who are you? Declare yourself," he demanded, though he felt foolish giving orders when he was naked and weaponless.

The man did not answer, but there was a flutter near his back.

*Oh my gods! Wings. Massive white wings.* Now that he looked closer, he could see that the shimmery light had settled about the man's head like a halo.

It really was an angel.

"I must be dead, then," he murmured, accompanied by a few Norse expletives.

"Not quite," the angel replied, "and if I were you, I would watch thy mouth."

"Chastened by an angel? Ha, ha, ha! Where are my seventy virgin Valkyries to welcome me to Valhalla?"

"I told you, Viking. You are not dead yet. And besides, there will be no virgins where you are headed."

*Uh-oh!* "Who *are* you?" He deliberately toned down his belligerence. A good soldier knew when to pick his battles.

"St. Michael."

Although he worshipped Viking gods when it suited

his purposes, Vikar had been baptized in the Christian church . . . a convenience practiced by many Norsemen traveling to far lands. As a result, he knew a little about the One-God and His followers. "The archangel?"

The angel nodded. "Some call me St. Michael the Archangel."

"Slay any dragons lately?" Vikar quipped.

The angel did not smile. "St. George does all the dragon slaying these days."

"Oops! So what are you slaying? Toads?"

"Best you ponder your fate, Viking, instead of making jests."

*No sense of humor.* If Vikar could laugh at this horrible situation, why couldn't the angel? But then he had no idea what his situation was. Frowning, he tried to imagine what had happened.

"Think, Viking," Michael said, as if he could read his mind.

*Hmm. I better not insult him in my thoughts.* "Last I recall, I was in the midst of a *holmganga.* That is a form of duel fought on a cloak. Whoever steps off the garment is considered a coward. Whoever wins such a fight to death gets all of the loser's property, including his women."

Michael made a snorting sound of disgust. "You cared only about Jarl Gaut's comely wife, whom you wanted to add to your many concubines."

Vikar shifted uneasily from hip to hip. In truth, he had realized just before the duel began that Bera was newly wed to Gaut and fancied herself in love, but by then his pride was great. He could not withdraw the challenge.

Besides, a little tupping never hurt any woman, even if she was marriage-bound to another.

"Can you hear yourself? Do you honestly dare to justify your actions thus?" Then more softly, Michael added, "You were not always so black-hearted."

Suddenly, into Vikar's mind came an image of his first wife, Vendela. It was their wedding ceremony. She had been fifteen to his seventeen. Sixteen years back, it had been. And what a joyous occasion! He a smitten, newly blooded warrior, and she with adoration in her clear blue, virginal eyes as they stood under the bridal canopy.

"Your heart was pure then, Viking." With a wave of the angel's hand, a new image came into Vikar's mind. Vendela again, but now she was twenty-five, as he'd seen her last. With eyes closed, her face and body lay battered on the rocks below Lodi's Leap, the salt cliff.

Horror filled him, even now after five years. "Why would she take her own life?"

"Can you possibly be that thickheaded? You put Vendela aside for your viperous new wife, Princess Halldora."

The daughter of King Ormsson from Norsemandy was indeed aspish on occasion, but seductive beyond compare. She had insisted that no other wives be in his keep afore speaking her vows, and he had been obsessed with her at the time. Even so . . . "I would have given Vendela her own steading at the far reaches of my estate. There was no shame in that," he defended himself. "She should have seen the esteem such an alliance would give my name."

"Thoughtless man!" the angel said with a shake of his head.

Tears burned his eyes and almost overflowed. He could not remember the last time he had wept, if ever. *Oh, Vendela! I am so sorry.* But immediately he shook such weak thoughts away.

The angel waved his hand again, and a new mind picture came to Vikar.

His grand home at Wolfstead. A palace, many said with awe. No wood fortress had been good enough for him. No, with the wealth amassed from his amber trading, along with a-Viking for plunder, he'd insisted on a stone edifice, three floors high, with tapestries and finely carved furniture from far lands. All a monument to his success.

"A monument to your vanity," Michael scoffed.

The picture in his mind changed. The stone castle dripped with blood, and he saw clearly the ten men who had died in the two years it had taken to build the structure.

He sensed where this was going. The angel meant to guilt him. "They were mere thralls. Slaves' lives do not matter."

"Can you hear yourself, Viking?" Michael repeated, gazing at him with sadness. "I do not know what I was thinking when I pleaded your case. You are a lost cause."

"I am not," he argued, though for what he was not sure.

As if by magic, that Wolfstead vision was replaced

with his most recent memory. Was it only this morn? A blood-soaked cloak and a screaming female voice just before the heavens opened with raging thunder and lightning as he'd never witnessed before.

Had he offended Thor, god of thunder? He glanced up at the frowning angel.

"There is only one God," the angel roared.

He flinched, but then he straightened. If death was his fate, he would face it boldly.

"I went to God, fool that I am, asking that He give you another chance," the angel told him.

Vikar brightened. Not death, then? "What would you . . . He have me do?"

"For your sins . . . and they are grievous . . . you will do penance sevenfold. For seven hundred years, you will do my bidding against the armies of Jasper."

"Jasper? Never heard of him. Is he a Saxon?"

Ignoring his question, the angel went on, "I will be the *hersir* of your soul."

*The chieftain of my soul? Pfff!* "Seven hundred years!" he exclaimed with outrage, but then an idea came to him of a sudden. "I would live for seven hundred years?"

"Sort of."

That sounded like a trap to Vikar. "And the alternative would be . . . ?"

"The fires of Hell for all eternity."

Well, that was certainly blunt. And he did so hate the thought of burning flesh, especially his own. "I agree," he said without hesitation, especially when a brief image flicked in his brain of a fiery pit with screaming creatures that must once have been humans.

The angel almost smiled. It was not a nice almost-smile. "Do you not want to know in what capacity you shall serve?"

Vikar waved a hand blithely. Seven hundred years was a very long time, but eternity in that fiery pit was unimaginable. "It matters not." He assumed he would be a warrior in some land of the angel's choosing. Perchance even a warrior angel.

"So be it!" Michael raised both hands on high, causing his wings to flutter and feathers to fly on a sudden breeze.

Then the most ungodly pain hit Vikar's face. It felt as if his jaw was breaking and all his teeth were being yanked out, one at a time. And on his back, a sharp object appeared to be hacking at his shoulder blades. When it was over, he found himself lying on the ground, felled with agony. As he rose to his knees, he glanced up at the angel with a mixture of anger and inquiry, but the angel said nothing.

Vikar reached over his shoulders where he discovered raised bumps, like healed scars, over his shoulder blades. His mouth felt odd, too, and was filled with the not unpleasant taste of blood. He ran his tongue under his teeth, which were . . . "Oh no! It cannot be so." He put fingertips to his teeth, which were uncommonly even and white . . . leastways, they had been in the past. Now two of the incisors on either side of his front teeth seemed to have elongated and grown pointy.

The angel had turned and was about to fly off.

*With all these questions hanging in the air?* "Wait! Fangs? You gave me fangs? Like a wolf?"

"No. Not a wolf." The angel did smile then . . . with glee. "A vampire."

On those ominous words, the angel disappeared.

And all Vikar could think was, *What is a vampire?*

Too soon, he found out.

### *Club Med for the undead . . .*

In a cold, cold, miles-long cave known as Horror, far below the surface of the earth, Jasper paced. It was not Hell, of course, but that place where Lucipires brought their victims before eventually sending them off to Satan's fiery pits, or to become vampire demons in Jasper's personal army.

"It is too much!" he railed at his assistant Sabeam, who raced to keep up with him. Being a mung demon, a species of full demon, unlike former Seraphim angels like Jasper or even prestigious haakai demons, Sabeam had limited status and authority, even with his massive seven-foot height. Then, too, there was the slimy, poisonous mung that covered every surface of its body.

"What shall we do, master?" Sabeam asked, puffing for breath.

The boy, who was only three hundred years old, didn't get enough exercise these days. Maybe Jasper should order him a treadmill.

"Satan demands his due," Sabeam told Jasper, as if he

didn't already know that. "We must send the souls to him as prescribed by demon law."

Unlike most mungs, Sabeam was not mute. Sometimes Jasper wished he were.

Still, Jasper nodded, knowing that he had no choice but to give up his collection soon. The last time had been two hundred years ago. This latest delivery was long overdue. "Grieves me, it does, to release my 'babies,' only to start all over. It will take us twice . . . no, thrice as long . . . to replenish the supply, what with the vangels hindering our efforts." Vangels were vampire angels that Michael the Archangel had created specifically to fight Jasper's legions.

He could not think at the moment of Michael, who had once been his friend. If he did, he would fall into the pit of despair that had held him the first hundred years of his exile.

Instead, Jasper gazed fondly around him at the life-size killing jars that held the newly dead human souls who fought wildly against the glass sides, to no avail. Once subdued, they were placed on display slabs with a two-foot pin through the heart holding them down. Like butterflies, they were, especially when they flailed their arms and legs in a wing fashion. Undead human butterflies that fought their confinement, eyes wide with horror at their fate. Jasper's own personal human butterfly collection. Playthings, really, that he liked to take out from time to time and torture. Thousands of them.

Most special of all was one of the few vampire angels they'd been able to capture, and that only a lowly ceorl,

David, who was stretched out on the rack at the moment whilst imps and hordlings, Jasper's foot soldiers of grotesque appearance characterized by oozing pustules, danced about the body, piercing the skin with white-hot spears, wrapping barbed wire around the always erect phallus, jamming odious objects up the anus, stuffing imp offal in the mouth. "Good work, Fiendal," he said, patting one of the hordlings on the head as he passed. "Do not go too far, though, lest the vangel get accustomed to the pain."

Fiendal nodded, his excessively long tongue lolling out with dripping drool.

Jasper continued his pacing, trying to think. As he walked, fury turned his face into icy shards that flaked off like scales. His eyes glowed bloodred, his fangs hung down almost to his chin, and his tail dragged behind him on the stone floor. He hated that his once-renowned beauty could be turned into this travesty of ugliness. Oh, he could transform himself into the most beauteous of humans, male or female, when prowling the earth. But this monstrous carcass was his true self now. And he blamed Michael for this most odious fate.

Long ago, before the world was created, he had been one of the chosen archangels until he'd been expelled from Heaven, along with Lucifer and all the rest of his rebellious followers. And it had been Michael, a fellow archangel, who had been the one to kick their unholy butts out of the celestial presence of God. Forevermore.

Now Michael was after him again.

For centuries Jasper had been sending out his special

creations, demon vampires, to the earth to bring in more doomed human souls in a faster, more efficient fashion than just waiting—*ho-hum*—for bad people to die. Horror was just a way station on the journey to Hell, but it was Jasper's own special playground, and now Michael threatened to take even that away from him by creating vampire angels to fight him. At the same time, Satan was demanding his due.

"We cannot continue at our present pace, one soul at a time. We must needs speed up the process. Bring in hundreds, no, thousands of doomed souls at one time."

"Like 9/11?"

"Holy Hades, no! God sent legions of His angels to Manhattan afore we could even arrive. Instead of Satan or I or any of the Lucipires being able to grab them, angels led them right and left to that holy place of which we do not speak. There were so many feathers flying about that day, it was a wonder the news media did not notice."

"Smoke," Sabeam remarked.

"Huh?"

"The feathers were hidden by the smoke," Sabeam said.

*I was kidding. Can a demon not even tease anymore? I am surrounded by idiots.*

"So, there is no event where you could harvest souls in large numbers?" Sabeam concluded.

"I did not say that." Jasper thought for a long moment as he continued to pace. Then he stopped abruptly. "I have the perfect idea. Did Satan not invent the Internet to blacken the souls of mankind?"

"I thought Al Gore invented the Internet."

Jasper rolled his burning eyes. *Can anyone spell* idiot? "It matters not who invented what, but how Satan uses human obsessions for his own ends."

"Okay," Sabeam said, though he clearly did not understand. No matter!

"We will prowl the Internet superhighway 'til we find the perfect venue for mass harvest of sinners all in one place at one time." Jasper would have licked his lips with anticipation if his frickin' fangs were not in the way.

## About the Author

SANDRA HILL is a graduate of Penn State and worked for more than ten years as a features writer and education editor for publications in New Jersey and Pennsylvania. Writing about serious issues taught her the merits of seeking the lighter side of even the darkest stories. She is the wife of a stockbroker and the mother of four sons.

Visit www.AuthorTracker.com for exclusive information on your favorite HarperCollins authors.